Final Vinyl Days

Also by Jill McCorkle

The Cheer Leader

July 7th

Tending to Virginia

Ferris Beach

Crash Diet, Stories

Carolina Moon

Final Vinyl Days

AND OTHER STORIES

by JILL McCORKLE

Algonquin Books of Chapel Hill
1998

Published by
Algonquin Books of Chapel Hill
Post Office Box 2225
Chapel Hill, North Carolina 27515-2225

a division of
WORKMAN PUBLISHING
708 Broadway
New York, New York 10003

Printed in the United States of America.
Published simultaneously in Canada by
Thomas Allen & Son Limited.
Design by Anne Winslow.

Some of the stories here originally appeared, sometimes in slightly different versions, in the following magazines and anthologies, to whose editors grateful acknowledgment is made: "Your Husband Is Cheating on Us" in *The Oxford American,* "Paradise" in *Chattahoochee Review* and in *New Stories from the South,* 1996; "Life Prerecorded" in Share Our Strength's *Writers' Harvest,* 1996; "Final Vinyl Days" in *Elvis in Oz: New Stories and Poems from the Hollins Creative Writing Program,* 1992, and in *It's Only Rock 'n' Roll: Rock 'n' Roll Short Stories* (forthcoming).

Library of Congress Cataloging-in-Publication Data
McCorkle, Jill, 1958–
Final vinyl days and other stories / by Jill McCorkle.
p. cm.
ISBN 1-56512-204-6
I. Title.
PS3563.C3444F56 1998
813'.54—dc21 97-50540
CIP

10 9 8 7 6 5 4 3 2 1
First Edition

For Shannon Ravenel
with great respect and thankfulness

And for Dan, Claudia, and Rob
with love

How many hearts have felt their world stand still?

Marvin Gaye
"If I Should Die Tonight"

CONTENTS

Final Vinyl Days

PART I

Paradise

When Adam met Eve they were standing in the champagne line at Missy Malcolm's wedding in Southern Pines. Eve, who had worn her thick black hair in a blunt Cleopatra cut since moving to Atlanta, had grown up with Missy in a small town just twelve miles away. In Atlanta she was Evelyn, an aspiring fashion designer and buyer for Macy's. But here she was Eve: Eve Lyn Wallace, a name selected by her paternal grandmother, who had once seen the name Evelyn in print and proceeded to spell and pronounce it in her own way. Here people voiced shock at how dark her hair had gotten since she moved to *the city*. Dark and straight. The woman in the pink knit dress who slipped a business card into the palm of any hand she shook—Gretchel Suzanne Brown, owner and head stylist of Shear Pleasure—stopped and fingered Eve's hair, saying over and over like a mantra, "I don't remember this hair."

Eve finally, in embarrassment, turned and explained all of this to Adam; she explained that when she was in high school she had a perm that made her hair lighter and quite frizzy. "Nobody around here gives a decent perm," she said, traces of the region's accent lingering on the syllables she attempted to clip. "And especially not her." She nodded toward Ms. Gretchel Suzanne Brown, who was working her way down the line to where the bride and groom stood.

Eve's eyes were catlike, almost amber colored in the bright banquet room. It could have been any country club anywhere, any random wedding, and Adam was struck by how alike they all were, the tables and flowers and fountains, the little bite-size pieces of food that after a while began to taste the same, the common ingredients being wooden toothpicks and miniature puff pastry shells. The mothers and grandmothers and aunts all decked out in pastel dinner-mint shades of chiffon. Eve was in bridesmaid's garb, a layered gossamer pink number that was identical to those of the other seven attendants, all of them wearing the little pearl earrings that Missy had given them at her bridesmaids' luncheon two days before, hosted by wives of the local dermatologists. Adam heard all of this while seated in the church waiting for the service to begin. The women (who were seated on the left, the *groom's side,* only because they ran out of *good* seats on the right) exchanged rave reviews of the scrumptious little delicacies served at the party: cucumber sandwiches, petit fours, and melon balls. They were shocked at how those young women spoke so openly about sexual matters, and wasn't it *clever* of the hostesses to give out those little samples of Retin-A for party favors. "If those girls are smart," one whispered—Adam leaned forward a little to hear her better—"they'll use the stuff right now before it's too late. Skin goes fast. Lord, how it goes." Then this same woman changed the subject to how she had not been awarded Yard of the Month because her neighbor had five dead cars up on blocks in his side yard. Adam sat back and flipped through the songbook in front of him until the organ swelled and announced that it was time for the show.

The procession was a lengthy one, a great-grandmother with a walker, a great-aunt in a wheelchair, the back of which was decorated with ribbons and flowers, parents, ten groomsmen, ten bridesmaids, a best man (father of the groom), a maid of honor, a matron of honor (pregnant, and thought by the women seated in front of Adam to be way out of line for having participated, even if she was the bride's sister). There was a short shiny-faced kid wearing a mini-suit and carrying a satin pillow and there was a curly-haired little girl strewing flowers onto the green-carpeted aisle. Then here came the bride, her spike heels piercing petals all along the way. The children's fakey smiles made them look moronic. The women in front whispered that they were *deliciously adorable, precious, precious things*. They said it was so very *special* that the bride and groom made children a part of the day. No children in the oven, thank you; only fully baked ones, please.

I'm Adam," he said finally, as the hair stylist floated to the end of the champagne line, stopping once to lift and test a strand of the maternal grandmother's hair. "You're Eve?" Several people standing in line snickered.

"Evelyn," she said. "I go by Evelyn, now."

"But she'll always be Eve to me." The woman behind them—a woman with her pelvis thrust forward and big white pumps turned outward—stuck her head up close. "I taught little Eve piano for years and years."

The Minnie Mouse woman disappeared momentarily only to pop out again to recall how Eve, at age five, had had a little accident just before playing "Get Aboard the Big Airliner" at the big recital down at the Junior High

School Auditorium. "Wet herself a teensy bit," the woman whispered to Adam, her breath laden with denture adhesive. She leaned closer and stared at him. "You don't look or sound like you're from around here. You must be one of the groom's guests."

Of all the people in that lengthy procession to the front of the church, Eve was the first that Adam noticed. In the first twenty-six years of his life, he never set foot in a church, and now he had done it for the fifth time in two years. This was, however, his first time in a Baptist church, and he was surprised by the stately room, the plush carpeting, and mahogany molding, the red velvet chairs like thrones. He had envisioned snakes slithering up and down rock-hard pews and signs saying *This way to eternal damnation* and *This way to everlasting life* in the same sloppy style he had encountered on the roadside: WATERMELLUNS, CANTELOPE, HUNNYDO.

Adam and John Jeffers had been fraternity brothers at the University of Maryland. The high point of their relationship had been the annual Burnout bash their fraternity held to commemorate a famous frat house fire. For four years the two of them worked on planning the event: bands, kegs, T-shirts. For four years they blasted their stereos and played pinball in the dank, beer-soaked bar near their frat house. For four years John was a part of Adam's life, his face a daily sighting. Now he was marrying a complete stranger, this woman with short blond hair and a church full of relatives. Marriage plans were incongruous with the postcollegiate lives his fraternity brothers *reported* they were living. And yet the invitations kept coming. He had been in two of the five weddings.

In Adam's world, weddings were held either in a temple or some nice gilded hotel banquet room, where women turned out in black sequined cocktail dresses that showed cleavage. At his first big Southern church wedding, he'd learned that a female guest who wore black to a wedding was absolutely tasteless. Wearing a black dress was almost as bad as wearing a white one, unless you were the bride. There's only one virgin on that day. At another of the weddings, a man had stepped out in a powder-blue dinner jacket with tails and sung "We've Only Just Begun." Adam thought he could just as easily have been in Las Vegas or on *Star Search*. So as not to start laughing he spent that whole service (all written by the bride and the groom with a little help from Elizabeth Barrett Browning and Kahlil Gibran) memorizing pieces from the program he'd been handed at the door. He could now quote from Corinthians and the Book of Ruth.

It was hard to concentrate during this prayer, a very

long prayer. Glancing around the packed room, he kept coming back to Eve (at that point she was still *the one with the thick black hair*). He was thinking about the grooms who had gone before John Jeffers, all seated here now, looking somehow old and washed out, wimped out. They seemed subdued, professional, lobotomized. Their wives looked fixed and powerful with their tailored linen dresses and little clutch bags. These marriages were walking advertisements for Talbots and Brooks Brothers. They talked about the mortgage and the dining-room chairs that were ordered. If they weren't trying to have babies right that minute, they were buying AKC puppies. It was like all these guys had hopped on a ferry and left Adam there at the landing. With each wedding the gap widened.

The preacher's prayer was well into its second minute when the groomsman standing by Eve—John's cousin —began looking a little questionable: pale, shaky, damp. And with no further ado, the cousin passed out cold. He fell face forward, pulling Eve and a small candelabra entwined with gardenias and ivy with him. A roomful of people (hundreds of people) heads bowed, eyes closed, missed this scene of a lifetime. She fell forward as gracefully as possible, her pink skirt momentarily hiding all but a slender white leg. The preacher was talking about trust and loyalty, the everlasting gift of faithfulness. Adam raised up out of his seat to get a better view. He watched her emerge from the folds of pink fabric, gracefully ease out from under the dead weight of the groomsman's arm, mouth what looked like "shit," and then stand up, perfectly still and by herself, staring straight ahead as if she didn't notice this postadolescent lunk sprawled in front of her. The preacher talked a bit more about the state of the world today and how important it was to have a partner, but by then the whispering had begun and people were peeping, one eye, both, until the final amen. Eve stood, shoulders back and eyebrows raised, daring anyone to link her in any way to the body at her feet, his face gray and slack against the carpet. During the vows someone from the congregation tiptoed up and, as inconspicuously as possible, checked his pulse and then rolled him under the front pew where his head rested next to great-grandmother's walker.

Now the groomsman cousin was standing in the champagne line with a can of beer. *Hair of the dog,* people were saying. Men in Lilly Pulitzer suits nodded to the nauseated-looking fellow with great respect and recalled the wild nights *they* had known at bachelors' parties. Adam's friends from college winked and grinned, elbowed him and others knowingly. Their well-rehearsed marriages seemed to force further exaggeration of male bonding, boys' nights out. Their women smirked with what was supposed to be great wisdom about these "boys will be boys" moments. It was as if these women had opened the cage doors and *allowed* their guys a little recess. Adam imagined the charges they would submit to their husbands: a diamond tennis bracelet, a trip to Barbados, a summer home, four babies. The price of freedom was exorbitant these days. So why was everybody biting the hook? Why were these reasonably intelligent, likeable guys *choosing* to acquiesce, their suppressed desires left to blow up at some occasional wedding party.

Adam thanked God he had not been a part of the fiasco known as the bachelor's party—men too drunk to stand peeing in a downtown parking lot, shaving John Jeffer's pubic region, writing *Help Me* on the soles of his shoes (which was visible to all when he knelt during the last prayer). "Those boys, those boys," John's mother murmured several times.

The bride and her maids were no better it seemed. Rumors circulated (and were later confirmed by Eve) that the bride had been stamped in butcher's ink with "Prime Cut" and "Choice Meat."

"Sally Snow's dad works at Winn-Dixie," Eve told Adam when he asked how they had gotten the ink. It was chitchat, small talk, right in there with the insufferable North Carolina June weather, his completion of Duke Law School and recent move to Washington, her aspirations of getting in the fashion world. "As a designer of course," she said. "I'm much too short for anything else." She laughed and handed him a glass. Adam was five nine and she easily was eight inches shorter, her hand half the size of his as they both leaned against the stone swan fountain that spit forth pink champagne.

"They all act so juvenile," she said, throwing down one quick glass of champagne and then getting a refill from the swan before moving over to the food. "And did you catch the guy I was standing with? The cousin from hell?" She raised her eyebrow again, let out a heavy sigh. "I told him not to close his eyes during the prayer. I could tell he had that sick as hell look."

"Best part of the service," Adam said and motioned her out into what people kept calling the solarium, a jungle of potted ferns swaying over white wicker tables and chairs and a big plateglass window that looked out on the pool and the eighteenth hole. "I particularly liked the way you got out of his hold. You did like this." He kicked one leg out to the side and held it there, shook it. The great-aunt was frowning at him from across the room where she sat hunched forward in her chair. He stopped a waiter and grabbed two more glasses of champagne and a handful of diminutive drumsticks. She eagerly accepted the champagne but turned down what she called biddy legs, so he went and found a waiter with caviar and another with fruit. He found a bottle of champagne in the kitchen and brought it to their table. Besides not being carnivorous she was not a fan of the tune selections given to the Casio player (all tunes Adam had heard on the accordian at every bar mitzvah he had ever attended, songs like "Spinning Wheel" and "Will It Go Round in Circles?"). They talked for at least a half an hour about the round/ring/circle theme in songs sung at weddings. During this time he verified that she was not married but also discovered that she was not *single*. An ideal situation for someone who is not *really* in the market. Back in Atlanta she had a person, friend, lover, significant other, current life partner, spousal equivalent. Again they laughed over all of the stupid names and she changed the subject to some local gossip, one of the old Lilly Pulitzer men, who, she told him, had once been picked up by the side of the interstate wearing nothing but his underwear. "And?" Adam asked, rolling his hand dramatically for the rest of the story. She shrugged. "That's all that anybody ever heard. Obviously you're not a local," she said. "If you were, you'd be used to half stories and numerous speculations."

He realized then that he'd given her very little of himself. "I *was* in a lengthy relationship," he had offered with the news of her significant equivalent so-and-so. What he hadn't told her was that that relationship was when he was a sophomore in college, that he had been a slow healer, that his own parents flipped out in their fifties after thirty-something years of marriage and went through all of the same arguments you'd expect from a much younger divorce. They fought over who should get Barbra Streisand's *Greatest Hits* and the *West Side Story* soundtrack, until Adam went out and bought duplicates; of course then they had to fight over who would get the new versions and the CD player that his/her *nice son* had been forced to buy with his hard-earned money and him not even out of school yet. It was one of those times he caught himself wishing that there was a sibling with whom to divvy up the worries, someone to call just to say, "So, what do you hear from the insane ones?" By then, Alicia was already out of his life, no more than a glimpse of blond hair and add-a-bead necklace in the undergraduate library or at a basketball game. Where he had once pictured her face in the scenarios of his future, there was now an oval blur with a voice all too similar to his mother's and Great-aunt Izzy's, whose claim to fame was that she had once seen a very famous actor (she never revealed who, just that he was *not* Jewish) buying every kind of laxative that was stocked at her local pharmacy (which of course was *not* "his" local pharmacy). Every family gathering was punctuated by questions like "Was it Cary Grant?"

"Oh no, much sexier."

"William Holden?"

"Shorter."

"Frank Sinatra?"

"You think he's sexy? Do you really?" Izzy had the habit of nodding while she talked or chewed. Sometimes she did all three. Alicia had once guessed Marlon Brando, to which Izzy laughed hysterically. "I have never found him to be sexy!" Izzy roared. Not long after this, Alicia broke things off (it was as easy to blame Izzy for the breakup as it was to come up with any other good reason), and when Alicia left, Adam more than ever relied on the eternal brotherhood made available by Pi Kappa Alpha; he drank beer and shot pool, played pinball, threw darts, cochaired the Burnouts.

Now he realized Eve was staring at him. She had refilled both their glasses and was tapping her fingers to the beat of a jazzed-up version of "Mrs. Robinson." People were trying to dance to it but seemed to be failing miserably. One man in the center resembled a disabled turkey, all movement taking place in the head and upper torso. "I just moved to DC." Adam was suddenly determined to give something back to the conversation. "I grew up in New York. My parents are still there." He didn't offer that his parents didn't speak to each other except through him, that they had succeeded in making his life miserable.

"Atlanta." She lifted her glass for him to refill it. "I moved there right after college." She paused and laughed. "No big deal *now,* but back then I had never been anywhere. You know I lived at home all through college, small school close by." She threw her thumb over her shoulder as if he could look out into the foyer of the country club, the gold-flocked wallpaper and chandelier, and see her school. "I did *not* know anything about anything." She used her hands dramatically as she enunciated each word. He imagined her standing in front of a mirror as she clipped the slow-motioned syllables, as she avoided contractions like "didn't," where her native tongue pronounced *ts* for *ds*, "ditten" like "kitten." Then she brought in the hands, graceful, nubby-nailed hands that moved with great energy as if she might suddenly burst into applause or grab you by the throat. As with her half-baked stories about the people from her town, Adam had no idea where her conversation was going. He wanted to tell her that he liked the stripped-down version of her: that image of someone about to go somewhere, Little Eve Wallace with the frizzy hair, peeing at the piano recital, growing up to go to what sounded like a community college, growing up to be the first person he had felt any strong interest in since Alicia, but then he remembered that nameless, faceless significant other opening her refrigerator, watching her television, lounging on her bed down in Georgia. What he pictured was the face of Tom Cruise on the body of Arnold Schwarzenegger; as smart as Einstein and as sensitive as Alan Alda.

Look, it's Adam and Eve," the goofy-looking little ring bearer said, and several guffaws and titters followed. It was clear he had been put up to it. Apparently, their socializing had sparked quite a few Adam-and-Eve jokes, the punchlines all having something to do with a rib or a snake. Apples. Fig leaves. Then there were jokes about the company, Adam and Eve, that manufactured all kinds of sex toys and devices, the kinds of things the boys gave John Jeffers after his shave and the girls gave Missy Malcolm after her stamping.

"So you grew up here?" he asked. They had moved over to a table near the window—like a wide-screen movie—to escape all the traffic, and now they were watching people walk up from the eighteenth hole, swimmers pulling themselves up the pool ladder and adjusting body parts. She continued her commentary on people at the reception: the woman in a purple sarong had once chained herself (along with her two dachshunds, Oscar and Meyer) to the door of the local veterinary office to protest pet euthanasia (her husband was an anesthesiologist who was at that time being sued for overgassing someone); the couple making out in the corner had built a relationship and marriage upon dramatic breakups and reconciliations (like the time they were caught having sex behind the shower curtain display in Wal-Mart); the man stuffing chicken livers wrapped in bacon in his mouth had taught her high school geometry class and was the first person in town to come out of the closet. A few people came over to try and get in on the conversation, to ask her to dance, or (she said) to check up on them, but eventually they were left alone. An hour into the reception and people stopped asking.

"They will be saying all sorts of things about us before long," Eve said. "Here's the half story. We have spent the entire reception all alone drinking champagne: you, the out-of-town stranger, me the local yokel who *supposedly* has a man in *the city*." She lowered her voice to simulate danger.

"Supposedly?" Adam asked. "Are you asking me to speculate?"

Off to the side, the pool shimmered and children screamed and cannonballed and teenage girls lounged in bikinis catching the late afternoon rays. In the main room the champagne swan had gone empty, and bottles were being brought from the kitchen and passed around. The young black man on the Casio was singing "Sunshine of My Life." He put on some sunglasses and moved back and forth like Stevie Wonder, which delighted the old people hugging the wall as well as the youngsters who were periodically appearing and then quickly disappearing with shaving cream and soda cans. He sang *you are the apple of my eye* while the parents of the bride twirled and dipped.

Eve talked more freely now, and with that freedom came the accent, the slow drawl familiar to everyone else in the vicinity. "My dad grew tobacco, not much, but enough." She was home for a long weekend and, in the midst of giving her family history (two younger brothers and a mother who teaches fifth grade), she began describing her room there, the tape marks on the pale yellow walls from where she had hung posters in high school. Posters that said things like "Rain Is a Freedom Song" and "Up with People." She described her parents: childhood sweethearts who had developed a whole language with eyebrows, winks, and hand gestures. She described the cool, soothing feeling of the central air conditioning and how she had spent much of her childhood without it. "My brothers and I used to sleep on the screened porch floor in our underwear." She laughed, staring out at the pool now as if she could see her young brothers standing there in their briefs. "And my dad would take us out to the little local airport on Sunday afternoons to see if a plane came. You know little planes, crop-dusting types." She talked faster and faster, her neck and chest flushed. "We'd spread a blanket and count jets, which of course did *not* come to our airport. My dad said, 'Look, they've scarred the sky.' I always liked the sound of that, *scarred the sky.* And sometimes we'd stay until dusk and count the bats that flew out from an old barn nearby."

The lazy haze of the sun, the alcohol, her voice were getting to him. The smell of chlorine and the slow whirring of the ceiling fans. He was thinking about his room at the Ramada Inn, how dark those heavy, lined drapes could make it, how the unit on the wall could generate the artificial coolness. He couldn't help imagining her there with him, and once he'd let the forbidden idea in he couldn't shake it.

"Who looks stupid, us or them?" she asked, a mere second after ending the airport story (how they always stopped at the Tastee Freez on the way home, and how her youngest brother always asked if you could order a sundae on any day other than Sunday). For the first time he noticed the slight space between her front teeth, the little whistle sound she emitted with each and every *s*. It made his chest ache just to look at her.

"What do you mean?" He took off his coat and found his arm stretched out behind her, his finger lightly brushing the spaghetti strap of that hideous dress that looked amazingly good on her. He was now of the belief that anything would. She could grab one of those starched old-lady dresses and whirl around a few times, and it would look perfect: soft and easy and lived-in. She could wear the tablecloth, the ivy trailing from the centerpieces. He waited to see if she would move away from his hand, but instead she leaned in closer.

"Well, there they are in bathing suits." She lifted her hand with the champagne glass, index finger pointing outward. "And here we are in formal wear." She had kicked off her shoes and had her legs stretched out, ankles crossed on a chair.

He was about to make a flirtatious suggestion, something that she wouldn't necessarily have to take seriously, when there before them stood a plump twelve-year-old, her own spaghetti straps digging creases into her sunburned shoulders, handing out little net sacks of rice. It was clear to Adam, having observed all of the bridesmaids at the front of the church, that Missy had chosen the dress with Eve in mind; she was the only woman there who could do it justice.

"Believe it or not," Eve said, shaking her head with a lovely look of pity on her face, "there was a hell of a lot of thought that went into what just happened." At first Adam thought she had read his mind, and then he followed her gaze to the kid with the rice. "The girl, that basket with the streamers that match our dresses, and the great-aunt's wheelchair," she laughed a little too loudly and then patted her lips as if to reprimand herself. "The net cut exactly the right shape and sewn up, the Comet rice dyed the right pale shade of pink."

"They dye the rice?"

"Of course." She touched his arm, lightly fingered the fabric of his cuff. "What, you've never dyed rice? Lived all these years and you've never dyed rice? It's a big deal, this dyed rice. The only thing hotter is birdseed." Now her hand was curled up on top of his, and it was perfectly natural for him to turn his wrist and lock fingers with her. She talked faster as this was happening, all about birdseed for the environment, nobody has to come and sweep it up. She had told Missy all about this, all about how every wedding she had gone to in Atlanta had had birdseed, but Missy was just so traditional she had to have rice. "She even wanted to go to Niagara Falls!" Eve attempted a whisper but failed. "Donna Reed is her idol." Eve held one of the little napkins that said "Missy and John" up to her mouth, shoulders shaking with laughter as she continued the appraisal of her friend. "She knows how to make seven different meatloafs, loaves, and forty-seven things to do with Jell-O."

"No lie."

"No lie." She squeezed his hand tightly and moved closer, their foreheads almost touching.

"Sounds a little kinky."

"No shit, Jack." Clearly she was not entirely sober, and he caught himself hoping that the glassy-eyed haze would never wear off, that they could just step out into the bright June day and walk off into a perfect world. "You know, I meant Donna Reed as she was on TV, of course, with the Jell-O and meatloaf, you know. Donna in real life was really cool, protested Vietnam, thought women were capable of a hell of a lot more than that show made it look like, you know? Donna was okay."

There was a lot of activity outside, and they stood and looked out the window just in time to see the groom lifted and hurled into the pool, a herd of children in bright suits and water wings scattering so as not to be hit by the big drunk man and all of his tuxedo-clad groomsmen and two bridesmaids who followed. Eve said that the local rental place was used to this. She had been surprised when attending weddings in Atlanta that every groom didn't *always* get thrown in the pool. It was a ritual around here, had been forever.

"Are we being antisocial?" Eve asked as the groom stood by the pool wringing out his coat. He pulled wet money from his pocket and fanned it in the air. It seemed most of the people had gone outside to watch. The singer had packed up his keyboard and was getting some food from the sparse table. They had missed the cutting of the cake, and now the little plastic bride and groom along with two doves and a big silver heart perched on the upper tier reigning over a messy, half-eaten cake.

"Oh," he said and let his other arm drop around her waist, the light pink fabric cool and slick. "Are there other people here?"

It took forever for the bride and groom to come out for the big farewell. Many people had already left the reception. Supposedly, all the bridesmaids were going to help the bride get dressed, but Eve said that she thought they could do without her. The result was lots of people whispering "Where is Eve? Where is Eve?" so that someone else could say "Oh, of course, with Adam."

By now the biblical humor had been reduced to a lot

of snake jokes. The mothers and grandmothers and aunts were tired and flat, eyes dulled by the champagne they had pretended not to drink. Missy's parents wept openly as she turned and whirled her bouquet, which was caught by a middle-aged man in a bright yellow suit. Adam confessed this was unfamiliar to him, these men in fluorescent colors, that they should be required by law to pass out sunglasses.

Everyone cheered when the car drove away, and women pretended not to see where someone had written *get some* in shaving cream.

One of the grandmothers pointed out to all the guests the delightful message "Come again and again." Adam and Eve both said good-byes to the remaining people they knew, both complimented Missy's parents on the lovely wedding. And then they were left there, in the parking lot of the country club with the heat weighing down oppressively. Eve was swinging her shoes by her side, her other hand still clinging to his. "Well," he finally said and looked off into the pine trees surrounding the tennis courts. "Would you like to go get something to drink? Eat?"

On the ride to the Ramada Inn he regretfully had to let go of her hand to shift gears. She talked in great bursts of speed, much information delivered, such as that she would have to go back and get her car, her parents were expecting her for dinner, her feet were killing her, and then she fell silent. He was worrying about what to say next, what to do. It seemed that the force that had brought them together was dwindling and he didn't want that to happen. He pulled into a parking space, killed the engine, reached over, and took her hand.

The rest of the afternoon passed slowly in the cooled, darkened room, in the light of the muted television as the weather channel continued its ceaseless forecast—Washington, Atlanta, Kalamazoo. Her dress was crumpled in the corner, like some ghost of the Victorian era that had pulled up a chair to watch. Her unlikely underclothes, strapless bra and briefs in red-and-green striped cotton, were looped over the lamp that was bolted to the bedside table. He lay there watching her, trying to decide where to go from here. What did this mean? Were their lives irrevocably altered, or would they say good-bye and pretend it never happened? A long-distance relationship was the last thing he needed, that and an angry, hulking boyfriend, now standing seven feet tall with multiple tattoos and an arsenal. He had no desire to go through what he had just witnessed, this ceremony that might lead him right into his parents' life, the ultimate sacrifice, thirty miserable years thrown down the sewer for the sake of *the child's* well-being. But then again what *was* he waiting for? His own history offered none of the porch-sleeping comfort she had described.

The last thing Eve had said before dozing off was that he shouldn't let her sleep past four-thirty and already it was a quarter till five. He shook her gently and was greeted warmly, as if some part of her had not expected to see him there, and then she was in high gear, clothes retrieved and adjusted, fresh lipstick and mouthwash. He drove her to her car at the country club and, without meaning to, asked if he could see her again. Without breaking his stride or giving her opportunity to respond, he continued "and *if* I could see you, then *when*?" How much longer did she plan to live with this guy who obviously meant nothing to her?

During the next two months they met six times, once in Atlanta (the only trace of his predecessor being a book about transcendental meditation, a makeshift bong, and one really ugly polyester blend shirt, which enabled him to replace his Mr. Wonderful image with one that made him question her taste), once in Washington, and four times in a Days Inn in Greensboro, North Carolina. They talked on the phone every other day. Adam was starting to feel an obligation. Once he even thought the words *future* and *commitment.* He could foresee all the problems on the horizon: *where* would they choose to live? Would she even consider leaving the job that was going so well for her? God, would she have to have three children, just as there had been in her own family?

"You know this is never going to work," he said, his hand slowly pointing from her chest to his own to make sure he was understood. She was in his sparse apartment, her hair still dripping from his shower, which she had quietly mentioned was a haven for fungus; she was wearing the flip-flops he kept just outside of the bathroom door.

"Why?" She absentmindedly picked up the magazine she had brought with her. A woman in a tweed blazer looked up provocatively from the slick page. She angled herself, terry cloth robe tied loosely. "You mean us?" She said the word *us* as if it had been there forever, *us* like life, truth, God, eternity. He nodded slowly, and she nervously picked the magazine back up, riffled the pages sending the heady floral fragrance advertised there into the room. "Why?"

"I'm not sure." He went over to his CD collection and began flipping through cases. "I'm just not sure." What he was thinking was it's now or never. Either we're going to call it off, or we're going to make a decision. He was thinking that tradition says *she* should be the one initiating all of this and yet there she sat, calmly asking all of the questions.

"Is it the North/South thing? I mean I never said I have to always live in Atlanta." She waited, forehead furrowed while he shook his head. He had given up on the argument that DC was not "the North" and in fact was considered by many to be in "the South."

"Well, is it the Jew/Gentile thing? Because I really feel that I could go either way." She paused, mouth twisted in thought. "I mean I wouldn't exactly *broadcast* it at home."

"No. That's not it." Now he was thoroughly confused. He had no good reason. All of the likely ones were there, but they simply weren't good enough. They weren't good enough to overlook that rare match that might never happen again. How many awful weddings would he have to attend just to even come close to such a meeting? Still, he felt like a fool, confused and speechless.

"It's the Adam and Eve thing," he finally said later that night when she was almost asleep. "It drives me absolutely nuts."

"You're not serious?" She fumbled to turn on a light and then turned to face him. She was propped up there on her elbow without a stitch on, her thick hair fanned out around her face. "I was going by Evelyn, remember? *You* were the one who started calling me Eve. *Little Eve Lyn*

Wallace. Little Eve Lyn Wallace. You said it so often you sounded like a mynah bird." Her eyes watered, but she fought the impulse with a deliberate laugh and a forced shake of the head. He waited for her to deliver her biggest piece of ammunition, the fact that she had let him talk her right out of her old life and romance and right into his. He could hear it coming, the blame and insult, the imposed guilt and obligation. And then he knew. He knew that what he really wanted was for her to tempt him, seduce him, beg him to marry her.

"You are serious." She sat up and pulled her worn-out robe from the floor. She had announced proudly on her first visit that fashion should never forsake comfort. Now she was lost in the loose folds of terry cloth, the belt pulled tightly around her waist, and he found himself thinking about how she had said that as a child she had to sleep with her hand over her navel for fear that the bogeyman would come and touch her there. He realized then that he had already wrapped the blanket around his body like a cocoon. This was not a conversation to have naked. "What if we were Mary and Joseph?"

"They had better results."

"I have no intention of being the person you want to step in and ruin your life, be an excuse for you to be screwed up and feel sorry for yourself." Her speech gave way to the slow twang he adored. "I know that's what you're looking for, and that's not why I'm here."

Now he felt entirely stupid. He felt so incredibly stupid that he tried to turn it all around into a joke. She pulled out that big piece of hard Samsonite luggage that her parents proudly surprised her with (it was a story she often told when she had had too much to drink and was feeling homesick) when she moved to Atlanta, and he felt desperate. He begged her never to leave him. He said they should get married then, that weekend. He suggested they pull out the atlas and look up all of the Edens they could find—Arizona, Maryland, North Carolina, Texas, Wyoming. They could get married in Eden, North Carolina, or Eden, Maryland; maybe they would live there forever. Maybe they would go to Eden, Australia, on a honeymoon, or maybe that was a trip for later, maybe that was for the silver anniversary. He hadn't meant anything that he'd said; it had been anxiety talking.

She thought it was all hilarious for a while. She laughed and kissed him, said that he was sweetly weird. She said that there was no reason to rush into anything, that given all that he had been thinking, she felt it best to wait at least a few months and then talk it over again. This made him feel the need all the more; he said he wanted a standard wedding, everything and anything she wanted.

She said that she first needed to find an equivalent job; they needed to find an apartment with a clean bathroom.

When they finally got married, it was in that same country club on a June day just about as hot. The bridesmaids wore lavendar and there was a champagne fountain, but no one passed out and Adam did not get thrown into the pool. Gretchel Suzanne Brown did give out quite a few business cards, and there were many, many biblical jokes and great philosophical musings such as whether or not Adam and Eve had navels. Adam's fraternity brothers were threatening to strip him naked so as to answer this question as well as count his ribs, and he was praying to the God he wasn't sure existed that this wouldn't happen. If it did, people would see he'd been trapped, held down, shaved. He had not even told Eve. He was also praying her body would not be covered in blue ink when they returned to the Ramada Inn to spend their first night.

And one year, six Chippendale dining-room chairs, and one neurotic AKC-registered Irish setter later, while in labor with their first child, Eve made it altogether clear that she preferred to be called Evelyn whether he liked it or not, that she was sick and *goddamned* (she gritted her teeth for emphasis) tired of the jokes, tired of him telling people that they met on the sixth day. It had been his way out, this ridiculous connection, as if by fate he had been forced to marry her. He was always the innocent one. Always the abused one, the neglected, the ruined man. She told him to put blame where he should, on his toilet training, his parents, his obsession with names, and to tell somebody who gave a damn, like a psychiatrist. She was seized by another labor pain and proceeded to say every word she had ever read on bathroom walls, the slow accent exaggerating the harshness of every single syllable.

"What about Cain if it's a boy?" Adam asked, trying to entertain the young nurse who after many bloody attempts finally got an IV in Eve's vein. Eve had pointed to the helpless young woman's head and screamed *Yoo Hoo! Stoooopid. Anybody home?*

"Cain," he said again. "Now, there's a good strong name from the Bible that you don't hear too often."

"You don't hear Judas too much," the nurse whispered and stifled a laugh. Thank God, Eve had her bare back to them at the moment and missed that exchange; she was saying "shit" through clenched teeth over and over in the rhythm of "Jingle Bells."

"Judas, I like that," he whispered and then went back to his normal voice. "But Cain . . ."

"If I'm alive," Eve screamed in anger. "If I'm *able*, I'll name this little son of a bitch anything I please."

"Able, she said *able*." The nurse held her hands up to her mouth and fled the room.

Don't look back," he said two days later as they were leaving the hospital with Sarah Wallace Rosen, nothing marked or murderous about her. "You'll turn to a pillar of salt." They were in the parking lot, Sarah wrapped in a lightweight cotton blanket, the cloth shielding her face from the sun. "Wasn't that Sarah who turned to salt? Wasn't she Lot's wife?"

"I always thought they said *pillow* of salt," Eve said. "I always pictured something entirely different from what they had in mind." She swung around and stopped, stared at the doorway they had just left. "Still here," she said, "I guess we're not worthy of those biblical names after all," and Adam lifted the camera hung around his neck and focused: Eve pasted on a background of chain link, red brick, and shimmering black asphalt that stretched into parking lots and one-way streets, highways and runways, subdivisions and cocktail parties, fields, forests, temptations and promises.

Last Request

My mother's last words to me were "No matter what happens, no matter how lousy your life becomes, stick to your marriage, stay there, and *make* it work." I would like to have ignored her, but that was impossible, seeing as how she had eased out of a coma to deliver this message and there was a crowd of medical people standing around trying to hear her over the beeps and gurgles coming from her bed. My twin sister, Twyla, was right beside me, but of course she got *no* instructions whatsoever. All the dying demands were directed at me and *my* life with *my* husband, Doug Houston, *my* marriage of three years that I'd somehow bumbled my way into. Now she was trying to ruin it for me; minutes left in her life, and she was going for broke.

"He's better than I ever hoped you'd find," she rasped, her forehead bald of the sharp circumflex brows she'd been drawing on for years. Maybelline black-brow pencil nubs, years' worth, rolled around in her bathroom drawer along with my father's forgotten styptic pencils, lacquer-coated bobby pins, and loose aspirins. I couldn't even remember my father's face as I focused on hers, pinched and waiting.

"You were so right to marry him. Now promise," she hissed, her lips so thin and pale when stripped of the Revlon Rich Girl Red that she had worn since creation. Always, even at breakfast, it was already applied, marking her cup and cereal spoon with a greasy red film. Maybe she slept in it.

Promise. This is what happens when you are the responsible one. You are handed out huge demands while your recently divorced, let's-have-a-party kind of sibling gets a little pat on the hand to stop her violent sobbing. Twyla and I are fraternal (or sororal as our mother always said) and really look nothing alike. People used to say, "How can you be twins?" comparing her wee petite body to my size-thirteen hips, her thick dark hair to my do-nothing frizz. When people said how pretty Twyla (the prettier of the two, they whispered) was, they then had to give me a runner-up-Miss-Congeniality-like superlative (Tina is so smart, so capable, so solid and dependable—great childbirthing hips).

"Promise it, Tina," my dying mother said and somehow in all of her weakness managed to leave me feeling so burdened *I* could have died. "Swear to God that you'll stay with Doug for all eternity, that you'll do everything to keep him. Let me die knowing that one woman in our family made her marriage work even if it killed her."

Everybody was waiting for an answer. What was she sentencing me to? Never had she pushed me in the right direction. Never had she given me good advice. She was the one who wanted to iron my hair straight (like Twyla's) back in junior high school and scorched it, leaving it to smell so bad that Ronnie Stewart, who sat behind me in civics class, complained to the teacher. She was the one who suggested I wear a Sunday school outfit, complete with white patent-leather sandals, and sing "The Lord's Prayer" in the high school talent show—*Elvis got his start with the gospel*—while girls like Stacy Price and Yolanda Wallace wore tight bodysuits and did cartwheels and splits. Twyla (who had kept her talent a secret) came out in one of our father's suits. He had only been dead a month at the time of the show, and somehow that suit had survived the day our mother ripped through his closet and drawers and cut up all of his things with her electric hedge trimmer.

The last time that I'd seen that suit, my father and mother were going to a dance at the Jaycee Hut down on the river. It was just a week before he died, and my mother had been acting strange. She was always talking about the laundry, asking my father's opinion about the laundry, how often did he think she did the *laundry,* did he ever stop and wonder what interesting things you might chance to *find* in the *laundry.* She painted her fingernails bright red, and when she stood by the front door straightening his tie, it looked for a minute like she might just keep pulling it tighter and tighter until his eyes bulged and popped, but then he kissed her on the forehead and gently pushed her away. It was one of those moments you look back on and wonder.

I was sitting there in the high school auditorium in my white shoes, missing my father and wondering how Twyla'd saved that suit, given my mother's thorough nature, but then I was distracted by the red spotlight on Twyla. Her hair all slicked back like a man's, she began to lip-synch "Take a Walk on the Wild Side." Her friend, Pete Ray, who had a terrible reputation and had had it ever since he brought some glossy magazine photos to school in the sixth grade, was operating her little phonograph and cheering her on from back stage. He was so greasy-looking, if you threw him up against a wall he'd just ooze on down and leave a trail like a slug. You'd think my mother would have said something about *him,* but the only description ever doled out to Pete Ray was *son of a podiatrist.*

Of course Twyla didn't win; the teachers never would have allowed such a thing. First prize was reserved for Yolanda Wallace, who could pull both feet up and behind her head and then roll around on her back like a little beach ball. She did this to that song, "Afternoon Delight," a song that will always remind me of my father's death. Maybe Twyla didn't win, but she did *bring the house down.* For weeks afterward, that's what people said: that Twyla, what a card, she brought the house down, what a hoot. She came back to bow three times, and then when everything died down, Mrs. Rupert, the Latin teacher and my sponsor, put on the record of "The Lord's Prayer." Somebody at the back of the auditorium yelled out for a separation of church and state, but I kept singing. It felt like my white patent-leather sandals were glowing. Why had I ever listened to my mother? I wished the big ceiling light overhead would fall and crush me as dead as my father.

"You were just, just . . . ," my mother had me by the

shoulders, tears in her eyes. "You were an inspiration." She blinked with the words. "Just a sweet inspiration. And you!" She turned to where Twyla was standing with our father's jacket tossed over one shoulder, a little moustache penciled on over her upper lip, "You just brought the house down, honey. Why didn't you tell us what you were up to, little clown? Isn't she the clown though, Tina?" My mother, her Rich Girl Red lips stretching into a forced smile, leaned her head right next to Twyla. "Where did you find the suit, honey?" she asked.

It was after that that I decided the best thing I could do for myself was to always do the opposite of what my mother said. That's how I ended up going to college instead of getting in on the ground floor of Aunt Rochelle's *clothing business* like Twyla. This business was Aunt Rochelle and six of her cronies sitting around all day crocheting string bikinis. Some of the bikinis had little beads and things crocheted into patterns. Twyla's job was to carry them around from store to store and get orders. Both of the clothing stores in town had ordered. The big seller was the one with flowers on the breasts. Aunt Rochelle was expecting these suits to go national any day, and that's all she and my mother talked about; they talked about how sad it was I had gotten that degree in art history and had nothing to really show for it while *the business* was expanding into cover-ups and lingerie.

And, that's how I ended up with Doug Houston, who on first meeting, my mother said was *a little plain and dull and ordinary;* nothing like Twyla's fiancé, Ronald, a lawyer who wore a lot of jewelry, some of it looking like it weighed more than he did. While this conversation was going on, Twyla was standing there in the kitchen laughing. She was modeling her wedding dress, a low-cut sequined number with a train longer than my mother's house. Her wedding bra was crocheted out of the finest weight thread and had little seed pearls up the straps. Aunt Rochelle had made it herself.

My mother leaned forward and rubbed at a coffee ring on the kitchen table. "I want somebody good enough for you, baby," she said. "I want somebody like Ronald who can do nice things for you, take you places. I mean, you are not equipped to care for yourself in any way."

"Well, it's not because Aunt Rochelle and I haven't asked her." Twyla climbed onto the center of the table and turned to catch a glimpse of her whole self in the big picture window.

"What if you married that man?" My mother leaned to the side to see around Twyla's dress. There were flecks of midnight-blue mascara (the color she thought I should wear) on her Cover Girl–laden face. "I mean he's studying to be a construction worker, honey."

"I have a good salary as a teacher," I told her, "and Doug is going to be an engineer."

"Those who do can," Twyla said and adjusted her dress so that her breasts were pushed way up like Olivia Hussey's in *Romeo and Juliet*. "And those who can't, teach. That's what Ronald says." She stepped down onto the chair and then to the floor, her train sweeping the cowboy boot salt-and-pepper shakers that my mother had bought on her honeymoon in Nashville to the floor.

Ronald was such a prize. He slicked his hair straight back for what he called a Wall Street look. He drove a Grand Prix that my mother said made her feel *regal* when he drove the three of them to the Country Caboose where he said he *wanted* to order headcheese but got the brie crêpe instead. Twyla said that Ronald said that appearances are just about everything, and it seemed our mother agreed. Twyla breathed on her diamond, rubbed it on a dish towel, and bent over the catalog of bridesmaids' dresses on the kitchen counter. Her breasts were about to escape altogether.

"Engineer, huh," my mother said. "So, no wonder those little hands of his are always so clean. Just stand back and tell others what to do, huh? That explains all those big words of his." (He had once used the word *exacerbate* only to have my mother say that she'd just as soon he go ahead and say what he really meant, filthy or not.) Now she walked over and pulled up on Twyla's dress so that her breasts settled back down where they were supposed to be. "Your father was such a man."

"He was a fireman."

"That's right. A fireman," she said. "Which means, when you think about it, that he didn't work a day in his life. When has there been a big roaring fire in these parts?" She stopped and stared into her little laundry room. I knew she was doing inventory on all the different detergent samples she'd received in the mail. She loved samples and always had: soap, shampoo, toothpaste, but somehow she couldn't bring herself to use them; she liked to possess them, save them, count them. "When has there been a big fire anywhere in this state?" She stepped forward to rearrange a little tiny box of Tide. "He faked many fires, I know that."

"Ronald is a P.I. attorney," Twyla interrupted and continued talking right through our mother's telling something we had heard thousands of times, about how the fireman wives had discovered a big bonfire area out behind the firehouse where the men would go to get all sooty as a camouflage if they wanted to stay out late.

"When we first met at Singles Night I thought Ronald was a P.I., you know like Magnum, P.I." If Twyla had had any sense at all she would have been dangerous.

"No, sir," my mother continued, dabbing the perspiration from her hairline; her eyebrows were smudged against her shiny forehead, and sparkly blue eyeshadow creased in her lids. "I never could get the soot out of most of his belongings, Shout, Clorox, I've tried them all."

I wanted to say, speaking of fires, why in the hell is it always so hot in your house? But I held my tongue. It was so hot I thought I'd die. By then I had come to think of her as something that would grow and thrive under such conditions, like the spores of some kind of mold or fungus. Way back, I felt she was growing something bad, so I was not at all surprised when it turned out she had liver cancer.

"Those stains were symbolic," she said. "Oh, he might put out a little car fire out on the interstate," she said. "But he spent most of his time inspecting and demonstrating." She turned and laughed so loud that Twyla jumped. "Get it?" she asked. "That's what got him killed, all of that inspecting and demonstrating. He fancied *himself* a teacher."

"Well, those who can do," Twyla said. She had her eye on the bag of Hershey Kisses on top of the refrigerator, probably trying to figure out if she'd have time to run a few miles or do a couple hundred jumping jacks if she ate one. Thank goodness she had never gotten the hang of making herself vomit because she might have been very good at it.

"Answer her," Twyla ordered me, in a whisper. My dying mother was waiting, her eyes drooping and then widening with determination to stay awake; even in death she was the most stubborn person I'd ever met. Why was she doing this to me? What horrible thing could she possibly know about Doug that had made her want to approve of the union. I nodded slightly and then harder when she reached out to grip my wrist. I focused on Twyla, all dressed up for this visit. In the privacy of our own home, Doug and I called her *the little hooker.* She wore low-cut, lacy things, miniskirts, and spiked heels. Twyla was so thin it hurt to look at her. "What's the difference between a counterfeit bill and a girl who's anorexic?" Ronald asked us all one night in my mother's kitchen. He and Twyla were already having problems. Doug barely glanced up from the paper, politely gesturing that he really had to keep reading.

"Well, one's a phony buck," Ronald said, his arms opening wide in some gesture of confidence or ownership. "Get it?" Our mother had a blank look on her face, and I was trying to think of what I'd tell her the joke meant later that night when surely she would ask me. Ronald was drinking martinis to celebrate his latest whiplash case. Tomorrow morning he would sue a dentist for a faulty root canal, go to the chiropractor to whom he sent a steady stream of clients, and in the afternoon he would sue a family of five for leaving a roller skate on the front walk causing the fall of the realtor who had stepped onto their property to take a photo for a comparable file.

"He was trespassing," Doug said.

"All legal," Ronald said. He and Twyla looked like those little wind-up toys; they reminded me of those sets of teeth you can wind up and then let go, overbites chattering across table and floor.

"Trespassing." My mother was sitting there with the *TV Guide*. "Your father did a lot of trespassing."

"Forgive us our trespasses," Ronald said and strutted his way over to the martini pitcher. "That's from the Bible. I know a lot of Bible. You have to be well rounded to get into law school."

"It's from the Lord's Prayer," I said and then was sorry, because now either my mother or Twyla would remember to recount my singing in the high school talent show. There was so much of my life that I hadn't wanted to tell Doug about. I had never told him about seeing my mother in the laundry room that time, and I had never told him that my father made me wear a George Wallace banner and hand out bumper stickers outside of the Thriftway Grocery, which was where our precinct went to vote, and I had never told him that I sang "The Lord's Prayer" wearing white sandals and called it talent.

"That's right. And where is the Lord but in the Bible?" he asked. "Just where do you think the Lord is?"

"Not in this kitchen," I said.

I love you, Tina. Now swear to God," my mother struggled up a little from her pillow and squeezed my wrist. I didn't trust her as far as she could spit, which at that moment was no further than her bottom lip. I didn't trust Twyla, who paused in her sobbing to stare at a young doctor passing in the hallway. For what rose up in my mind now was the time I'd seen my mother standing there in front of her avocado-colored Maytag washing machine; I guess that was the only other moment I ever saw her completely stripped of her appearance, and it had left me feeling a little queasy and terribly sad, just like now.

I squeezed her hand, nodded that, yes, I would stay with Doug for all of eternity. She slipped back into sleep, her room a symphony of unpleasant sounds as the team of doctors, followed by Twyla, who was checking out all the left hands for rings, left the room. I waited until the door whined shut, and then I turned on my unconscious mother. "How dare you," I hissed. "You know something about Doug. You must. You have never pointed me in the right direction my whole life." Her eyes were closed, her mouth hung slack. If she hadn't been about dead, I might've slapped her, shaken her; before I could even launch into the humiliation of stinky scorched hair and performing a nontalent that set off a church-and-state debate, it was all over. As if at a green light (was there some such death beeper attached to her?) the people poured back into the room; Twyla collapsed in the corner, black lacy legs sprawled and showing way too much thigh. Somehow all the activity took on a rhythm in my head, the humming and bumping and beating. I was hearing the spin cycle of another time.

I spent the next morning taking care of Mama's arrangements, even though I was still furious at her for making me swear to God such a terrible swear. I felt myself studying every aspect of Doug, questioning every word that came out of his mouth. I tried to make him go on to work and leave me by myself, but he took it as an emotional outburst without real bearing and spent his morning opening the door to neighbors and friends of my mother's, who filled her living room with cigarette smoke and ceaseless talk of disease: tumors and masses and malignancies. They seemed to enjoy it so much I was afraid they'd never leave.

"That Doug's a doll," Mrs. Gladys White kept saying and nodding knowingly. She was one of Aunt Rochelle's crocheters, the one who had threatened to quit when Rochelle pointed out that her beading on the panties looked a little risqué.

"What did my mother tell you?" I asked Gladys White after about the fourth time. I pushed her right up against the pantry shelves, her head flush with a box of Quaker Oats Grits while I interrogated. I told her that I had heard all about that nasty, nasty, bathing suit she had designed. "You dirty old woman," I said, "you know something." I pulled on her little scarf by Vera just as my mother had pulled on my father's tie. Doug rescued her. He said something about stress, pressure, grief, and the whole time I studied his eyes for lies and deceptions; I sniffed all of his clothes in the hamper to see if I could smell quick afternoon sex. My mother had believed in signs and warnings, gifts from the great beyond. She believed that my father's death was fate, a grand scheme to bring justice to her life.

I was no sooner all calmed down when Twyla came over, dragging a man she had just met at the convenience store down the block from her house. She always has picked up people the way you might a loaf of bread. I studied him as he stood there in his Exxon uniform and imagined how he would affect Twyla's malleable personality. She would start talking garage talk: a cup of coffee would be a jump-start, a full tank; at the end of the day she'd be out of gas. "Why have you brought a date?" I finally asked her while Ted was in the bathroom. Her stare was so blank that I realized I was seeing what I'd never seen before—a moment when no one's light was being sent through her. I saw the void. Maybe my mother *had* tried to influence her. Maybe the suggestions just blew around in there and came out all twisted. Maybe there had always been people like Pete Ray or Ronald, P.I., or the Exxon man to get to her first.

It was a Wednesday morning when I saw my mother there in front of the washing machine. It was a day just like what's become in my memory the typical day of my adolescence. The house smelled of bacon and Pledge, the heat from within clouded the windows, and my mother stood before the window with the fire prevention safety tips decal on it and sorted clothes. Lights, darks, solids, lights dark solids. There was a pile of underwear at her feet, covering *her* white patent-leather barefoot sandals. Her painted lips turned down as she worked. I came upon the scene, unknown to her. She was holding a pair of size forty, ratty-around-the-edges boxers. A flash of red clung to the leg of the shorts, a red as red as my mother's lipstick. She pulled the thing off and then stood there staring into her open palm. Her eyes went blank and flat, as blank as Twyla's do, as fearful as a child's, and then her head started shaking. There was recognition, rapid nods.

It was not until my father was dead that she told this story, told how she had found a Lee press-on nail clinging to his underwear. It all fell into place for her then, she said, the knee-high hose she had found in the floorboard of his truck, the skimpy black tank top she found in the duffel bag that he took to and from the firehouse on his duty nights. She told us he'd explained these as little jokes planted by the boys. She told us she'd said, well, she sure didn't think of knee-high hose as some kind of sex item. Oh that, *that* was related to real business, that little rolled-up piece of dirty nylon belonged to an elderly woman who had broken her hip and called the department for a lift to the medical center.

"Can you believe it, girls?" my mother had asked us many times. "Can you believe what a son of a bitch fathered you?" This was right after we'd watched her being interviewed on the six o'clock news and just before she and Aunt Rochelle cranked up the hedge trimmer. "I don't see how the nail stayed there," Twyla said. "I mean I've used Lee nails, and I sure would feel it if one was to rip off that way, you know?"

But there was something wrong with that picture of my mother in front of the washing machine. Was it that it was a rerun? Had I seen it before? A long time back, when her hair was cut in a soft chin length and her make-up was sparse and clean-looking, I saw her in that same spot. She was wearing yellow shorts and a white midriff top. The fire rules showed behind her on the window while a big man with hair that ran down his neck leaned into her. This man stood still, moaning as my mother catered to him, her hands pressing the front of his trousers. As a child I thought he was deformed and in great agony. I thought *my mother helps the needy.*

The night after my father died, I wanted to ask who strayed first, but by then Twyla was crying on the phone to her latest boyfriend, who was being kept a secret (except for the clue that he was a big Lou Reed fan and his daddy worked on feet), and my mother and Aunt Rochelle were hanging clothes all over the house so that they could lop off a particular part of each item. There goes an arm. There goes a crotch. It was a little disturbing.

My mother had at hand all the reasons as to why my father deserved to go out with a freak stroke of nature, a sudden storm spurring tornadoes that touched down without any warning. He had said he was going to play a little golf with the boys since the forecast was for such a clear brisk day. My mother always said she had spent years trying to catch him in the act, and *in three seconds a big gust of wind did it* for her. It was appropriate, the perfect choice.

She never forgot to mention the time he drove us way out into the country to show us the *damnedest* thing he'd ever seen: a huge oak tree in the middle of a tobacco field, split through the middle with a precise blackened stroke. He explained that lightning had done it. I looked at the sight, the charred limbs against the then bright blue sky, and was struck by the contrast. I was proud that my father had brought us, that he was excited just the way he was when he used to take us to the Dairy Bar for a sundae. "Wow, Dad," I said, but that was before Twyla looked up from her *Archie* comic and screamed, before I saw the cows, their stiff frozen legs sticking out from them, in the shade beneath the tree. There were flies, too, in a thick black swarm.

"You see," my father spoke with authority. "The lightning went down into the ground and came out through the roots." It was the same voice he used when he let kindergartners slide down the firepole. "Now the bull, that smart old bull." He pointed off to the far edge of the pasture where the old brown bull, head lowered and horns shaking from side to side as he grazed, "That old bull knew that he should not come in from the rain."

"How smart." My mother said and fanned herself with the comic she'd snatched out of Twyla's hand. "Isn't the bull just so so smart." She reapplied her lipstick, and then turned back to him. "I suppose he'll just hop off to a new pasture and start over, huh?"

I was the only one looking back as we drove away, the bull seemingly unaffected by the fact that he was grazing in a death field.

Aunt Rochelle came over as soon as she heard about my father. The first thing she did was compliment the floral Qiana jumpsuit my mother had purchased for me at Bargain Wear USA. The second thing she did was tell how she had been widowed twice (like none of us knew by heart the intimate details of her life) and so knew how to take care of things like wills and a dead man's clothes. My mother said she didn't want his old underwear and socks left there in the drawer or his old shirts and mess left hanging in the closet, especially the tight polyester pants he bought for himself right after he saw *Saturday Night Fever.*

"If I were you, I'd burn this crap for fear something is crawling around in something." Rochelle stood there with her long brown cigarette up near her cheek. "I mean considering how and *where* he died."

The day my father died, the weatherman was on the news all afternoon, more or less apologizing for his error. His name was Joe Johnson and he was all right, curly blond hair and a nose a little off to one side, like a hockey player. Twyla decided she would write in and ask for his autograph. My mother said she certainly intended to write him a card and might even send a leftover floral arrangement.

Channel 11 ran the footage of my mother as she stood in the rubble being interviewed over and over. Just ten feet away from where she'd stood with the microphone in her face was my father's naked, sheet-draped body. She had come to identify him, with an abrupt *yep* at "the scene," as they kept calling it. My father was stretched out on the ground between a toaster oven and a fluffy piece of pink insulation. They told her there was no reason to announce that my father was naked, but she disagreed. She told them that the truth should be fully exposed.

As the three of us watched, she said she sure wished she had worn something different to go on television. But who would've thought that morning when she put on her yellow knit gardening shorts and matching shell, that within four hours—just barely after lunch—the sky would turn black and the wind would start whipping like the end of time. Who would've thought that when that infamous tornado sound—like a locomotive—hit my father's ears, he'd be bathing in the afterglow of . . . whatever.

My mother said she felt a rush of gooseflesh watching "the scene" on TV. She said it wasn't what had happened to him; nothing he did surprised her. No, it was the sound of her own voice, flat and slow, hitting her own ear. "Well," she said to the TV camera and gestured over to where his body was. "I sure didn't know he was here, if that's what you're asking." She pointed to the girlfriend who was all asob and riffling through her belongings. "Ask *her* what my husband was doing here naked." The girlfriend froze, her hands full of silverware, toilet paper stringing from her spikey high heels. She'd seemed more upset about her parakeet, having burst into violent sobs when she found its little body had been flung from the face of the earth, feathers all over the misshapen cage door. "It's not funny," she'd said and shook that cage at my mother.

"I've got your knee-high hose right here," my mother answered and held it out to her. "I got your Lee press-on nail. I got your sleezy old tank top."

"I don't have a tank top," the girl answered even though she was wearing one. "So there!" She stuck her tongue out at my mother, and they went to a local commercial for Stiles Chevrolet.

My mother had been lowered into the ground right beside the man who had made her so miserable. I kept trying to picture her again that day in front of her washer, to picture the man there moaning and arching and carrying on in front of her. Was it love or desperation or revenge or some strange combination of it all that she was feeling?

Though Twyla was traipsing to the cemetery nearly every single day with candles and rocks and roses, I kept my distance. Nearly a month passed before I got up my nerve to go out there and when I did, I was struck by how small and plain her headstone was, how the mound of red earth was already flattened by recent rain. It was a beautiful Saturday morning, the September air cool, invigorating. Doug had gone to play golf, and I caught myself thinking as I had been ever since my mother died: *he said*

—he *said* he was going to play golf. I could not trust a word from his mouth, and I was about to tell my mother just this, tell her how she had ruined my life, and why couldn't she have just died in silence instead of using her last breath to put a hex on me, when I glanced out toward the old pecan tree near the junior high school and saw that there were dark clouds gathering, a storm coming. I thought of that old bull grazing in his field, and I thought of my father more or less grazing in *his* field, and I thought of Doug walking from tee to tee, the tallest thing on the green—a warm-blooded lightning rod, and I was up and running to the car, and then speeding through town. I thought of my mother in front of her washer, younger then than I was now; I saw her lineless face, the pale brows she darkened to enhance her wide blue eyes, the frizzy hair she pulled so hard over big, bristly rollers. She wanted straight hair. She wanted barefoot sandals. *She* wanted a man like Doug. I pressed the accelerator a little bit harder, anxious to see him gathering his belongings and fleeing the approaching storm, a man smart enough to come in out of the rain. I could not wait to see him, to touch him. I would gather his wet clothes and throw them in the dryer where they would tumble and tumble and tumble, warm and dry when the cycle reached its end.

Life Prerecorded

When I quit smoking I dreamed of cigarettes. And when I was awake, cigarettes seemed omnipresent. They were everywhere: dangling from lips, burning in ashtrays. I felt the thin cylinder between my fingers, heard my words shrouded in fog, listened for the zip of a lighter, the scritch-scratch of a match. I could smell cigarettes from blocks away. Surrounded by hordes of people in the subway, I knew exactly who smoked and who didn't. I moved close to those who did, envying the habit, the rustle of cellophane in their purses and shirt pockets. I wanted to suck the stale tobacco from the fabric of their clothes.

I begged a cigarette from a complete stranger, a man

with dreadlocks who carried a brightly colored duffel (I didn't *look* pregnant after all), and ducked into a dirty public rest room, stood in a nasty stall that had no door, and read still nastier graffiti while inhaling and exhaling. And as I got down close to the brown filter (a much harsher brand than the one I'd abandoned), I kept hearing my doctor saying that he could tell which women smoked by the appearance of the placenta, and I could almost feel the poison I had just taken in settling like silt onto that little cluster of cells safely hidden from the world by skin, underwear, jeans, sweater, thick down coat.

The nurse who took my little cup of urine and poured it into a vial—another sample lined up with all the others waiting to go to the lab—didn't know how to arrange her face when giving results. A wedding ring is no guarantee. Age is no guarantee. It was easier for her to telephone, easier to deliver the news without a face, only monotone syllables: *Your test is positive,* confirming everybody's home stick tests, just like the one I had already tried twice. I found myself reassuring *her.* That's wonderful, I said, and I could hear her lengthy sigh at the other end. She faced a waiting room full of others: the young girl with mascara-stained cheeks, Clearasil and homework assignments in her synthetic leather purse, the one with some boy's ring and promise strung around her neck, the one who had no earthly idea how it could have happened.

The dreams started early, odd little snippets. I was at a table with friends, in a lively colorful cafe with hot-pepper lights, and I felt so jolly, robust and jolly, and when the cute young waiter, his hair slicked back like a flamenco dancer, came whirling by, I asked for another fruit juice concoction like the one I'd just finished. Delicious stuff. I ate the cherries and sucked the pineapples. I discreetly picked my teeth with the frilly little parasol. *Fruit juice?* he asks. *Fruit juice?* and the music stops, all heads turn to my table, to me, my abdomen clearly visible under a skin-tight top like nothing I have ever owned in reality. *Lady, you just sucked down your fourth double tequila sunrise.* What? *Lady, you look discombobulated,* he says with a shocked face and that word, *discombobulated,* with all its loud, harsh syllables seems to ricochet around the room. I get stuck on the word, my head bobbling, reeling, about to fall off. The images came to me, woke me, the blackened placenta slipping onto a clean hospital floor, the wide-spaced, staring eyes of fetal alcohol syndrome. That one was a recurring dream, right up there with the one where the bathtub is steaming and bubbly and this beautifully shining naked baby shoots from your hands like a bar of soap into the well of an empty tub or out an open window. There's the one where you leave the baby on the hood of the car and speed off down the highway, and the one where you accidentally pierce the fontanel, that soft spot, with something as innocent as the wrong end of a rattail comb.

There were times in those early weeks when I couldn't help but smoke. How bad could one cigarette really be? How bad could one little paper tube be, compared with nervous energy and honest-to-God craving? I walked blocks to a strange, distant neighborhood with a drugstore where no one would recognize me, to buy a carton, and then I hid them in the apartment, here a pack, there a pack, so it seemed like they weren't even really there at all. Early mornings, I stood in my nightgown and watched from our fifth-floor window until my husband disappeared around the corner. I climbed out on the fire escape with matches and an ashtray. The knowledge that I *was* going to smoke allowed me to slow down, take my time, angle myself so that I had a good view, red-brick buildings and sidewalks rising up Beacon Hill. Then I puffed furiously, the late November wind making me shiver as people down below scurried past in their down coats and scarves and hats. I watched our neighbor walking toward

Charles Street, his steps slow, as methodical as the metallic click of his prosthetic heart valve.

Our neighbor. As we were moving in, we had been told by the single woman below us—the one who wore faux-zebra spandex minis and catered to at least five Persians I could see lounging in her bay—to avoid *the old man* at all costs, to look the other way. He'll talk your head off, she whispered, and then rushed off to her job at a small gallery on Newbury Street. She never once asked what I did, somehow having gotten stuck in the groove of my husband's job (he's an actuary). Like many people who aren't sure what one *is,* she simply stopped talking and left.

I met our *old man* neighbor that same day while the mover was still bringing our things. It was only late August, but already it felt and looked like what I knew as the beginning of autumn in the South; there was a breeze off the Charles River and with it the sharp, water smell that I grew to appreciate, even to welcome, as home. The light seemed sharper, whiter, the shadows longer. It was a surprise to find that I *loved* this city, the street, the building. I thought about all of this sitting on those old concrete front steps, smoking one cigarette right after another—right out in public—and watching our belongings come off the truck.

It was while I was watching my Great-aunt Patricia's pie crust table angled and turned through the door that Joseph Sever stopped to introduce himself and then (as the other neighbor had predicted) proceeded to talk. He told me how he used to smoke, how he smoked Lucky Strikes, started during the war, liked them so much he kept right on. He said if he hadn't had such a good reason —his life— to quit, that he'd still be smoking three packs a day and enjoying every puff. But of course that was before his wife of forty years, Gwendolyn, died, before the heart valve, before his temples atrophied. He had been an accountant right there in the downtown area, and he described those April evenings when he worked so late, lighting cigarettes without even thinking, sometimes finding two lit and burning in the ashtray, as if he had an invisible partner.

He asked (it was clear he'd give consideration to any possible answer) how I spent my time. When he stopped speaking and there was a lull in the hoisting and heaving of the movers, I could hear his valve, a metallic click as it swung closed to prevent his blood from rushing back to its source. I told him that I worked as a copy editor for one of the publishers in town, and with that entry, he started in talking about books, his favorites from as long as he could remember: *Look Homeward Angel* as a young man new to the city, and then *Anna Karenina* and *For Whom the Bell*

Tolls, all of Hardy and Conrad, a little Jack London. "I'm a bit of a literary dabbler," he said. "I have written some perfectly horrible poetry myself." He liked T. S. Eliot and he liked Yeats. He liked to pause and quote a line or two with some drama, always stopping, it seemed, just as his breath gave out, at which point he tipped his latest L. L. Bean hat and bowed.

I came to learn that he purchased a new hat each season: the panama in the summer, the wool huntsman cap in the winter. I imagined a closet filled with hats, stacks and stacks like in that book *Caps for Sale,* a favorite book read in my memory in the voice of Captain Kangaroo. It turned out that at the end of each season, he continued to do what his wife had called *purging*. He gathered up everything he could live without and took it the Salvation Army bin down on Cambridge Street. "Everything except books," he qualified, "and of course the cats." He and Gwendolyn had always had cats, sometimes one, usually two. During his fifty years in the building, he had had fifteen different cats and could name them in one fluid motion, their names rhyming and rolling as each received an epithet: the friskiest of them all, the one with a terrible urinary problem, the one Gwendolyn never got over, the one who ate a rubber ball. He said that I should come visit his apartment and see what fifty years of books will look like.

"This will be your future," he said as he slowly mounted the stairs. "There are rows behind rows of books, in closets and in one very special kitchen cabinet. Gwenny always used *Heart of Darkness* to balance the lamp that wobbles by our bed." He paused on the landing before taking his flight to the second floor, the big brass-plated door propped open by the movers. "I keep it there. The lamp is a hellish thing, old and shorted out, but I keep it there."

I kept dreaming I was having a kitten. I looked at the faceless doctor and said, "Oh, thank God she didn't have her claws out." I told him that yes she was really cute, but that I was kind of disappointed. I really wanted a baby. At which point he laughed, just slapped his knee and laughed in a way that marked the absurdity of it all. *Imagine wanting a child.* Then I dreamed that I *couldn't* have a child, there was no child, and I went to a special clinic seeking help. I rode the T, changing trains twice; I took a boat and a bus and a taxi. The building was no bigger than the little drugstore around the corner and women of all ages and sizes and shapes were pressing up to the counter, behind which stood a woman in white guarding the shelves of test tubes. "Ah, yes, Mrs. Porter," she said and nodded when it was my turn. "We have your child." Suddenly all the other women were gone and I was being carefully handed a small glass tube. I held it up to the light and inside it I saw a beautiful little girl no bigger than Thumbelina, whom I remembered from my childhood fairy-tale book. She had dark brown hair that waved onto her shoulders and big blue eyes that I was absolutely certain I saw wink and blink in affection.

"Freeze-dried," the woman said. "Same process as coffee. Just go home and add a little water, you'll see." The woman looked like someone I knew, a former teacher, the mother of a classmate, I couldn't quite place the face. "Be very careful with her, now," she added and handed me a special cardboard tube, much like what you'd use to mail a stool speciman or a radon test. Carefully, I kissed the precious glass tube and slipped her into the sturdy container and then into the special zippered section of my purse. I put that into a brightly colored duffel and looped the strap over my head for extra security. In the dream I had dreadlocks and a joint hidden in my bra.

"Oh, by the way." I was almost out the door when I remembered the important questions I had planned to ask, all of the things that my husband and I had discussed before my long journey to this place. "Her medical history." The room was buzzing with grappling, grabbing women again, and I was being shoved out of the way. "Please. I really have to know all that you know about her." The woman seized my arm and pulled me behind the counter and back behind the heavily rowed shelves. She leaned close and whispered. Now I knew that I had never seen her before in my life. I would have remembered, the shiny broad forehead, the missing teeth. "You must never reveal what I'm about to say. If you do, people will want your baby. They will never let her alone." She leaned closer, her mouth covering and warming my ear as I strained to hear. "Her mama was Marilyn Monroe" she said. "And her daddy," she paused, looked around nervously. "JFK." I felt stunned, disheartened. Why couldn't my baby just be the product of Flo Taylor and Ed Smith from Podunk, Wisconsin? I didn't think to ask why they were giving *me* such a burden. *Is it all random, or have I been singled out, especially chosen?* My worries turned to mental health issues, sustance abuse genes, square jawlines, and prominent teeth. But then, because I was wondering about the rich and famous, I found myself thinking about good looks and talent and Southern roots. I dreamt I said, "Do you have one from Elvis?"

At three months, that magical time when you supposedly cross the threshold from morning sickness to a sudden burst of energy, the uterus slightly larger than an orange, we decided to take a vacation. The reason was clear. It was freezing in Boston, not to mention the fact that everywhere we turned people were saying to us, *Your life is about to change, it will never ever be the same.* Like birthdays, weddings, funerals, it seemed important to mark this transition, to remind ourselves continuously that something was in fact happening. We chose the Virgin Islands as a way of feeling we had gone very far and yet not left the country. I just didn't feel I could be pregnant *and* in another country.

The first day of our trip was like a perfect dream. I lazed in the sun, calypso music playing down the beach, the warm clear water as blue as the sky. I listened to the birds and the steel drums while I ran through lists of names in my mind—names of relatives long deceased. The voice of the man who was trying to interest my husband in a time share wove in and out of my thoughts. He'd sat himself down in his shorts and Hawaiian shirt, canvas shoes with laces untied, smelling like Hawaiian Tropic and some kind of musky aftershave, and asked my husband if teenage girls were better looking than ever before these days or was it just him? I heard him tell my husband that he preferred younger women, always had. "Like that one, mmmmmmm, mmmmmmmm," he said, his words oozing in such a way I half expected to see them like black oily leeches crawling off his tongue. I opened one eye to his gleaming white teeth just in time to follow his look to a string bikini, oiled brown thighs too young for cellulite. I wanted to sit up and tell him that of course he *liked 'em young,* that any grown-up woman with any sense whatsoever wouldn't touch him. But the warmth of the sun and the distant drums, the hunch that even the very young woman who had just passed would not give this two-bit Peter Pan salesman the time of day seemed satisfaction enough. That and the fact that I had lifted his almost empty pack of Marlboros and hidden them deep in my beach bag. I listened to him pat his pockets and look all around. Let him have a little nicotine fit, get a grip on the libido. I devised a plan: I would get up in the middle of the night and tiptoe out onto our balcony. I would huddle off to one side and blow my smoke with the wind just as I had done through screened windows of a locked bathroom as a teenager. A little mouthwash, deodorant, hairspray, cologne. If no one saw me, if I didn't confess, it'd be like it never happened.

The next morning I woke to the sensation of wetness, startled out of sleep by recognition as I hurried to switch on the fluorescent light in the bathroom. It was real; I was bleeding. Slowly, carefully, I called out to my husband and lay on the cool tile floor. I felt detached, as if I were in someone else's room, on someone else's vacation. I imagined a honeymoon couple, whirling and dancing, drunk and giddy, collapsing on the bed while the stark sunlight and still blue sea lay beyond the sliding-glass doors. Same place, same room, same toilet, different life. I lay there and questioned everything. Why did I buy the crib so early? Why did I smoke that Marlboro Man cigarette? I lay there wishing that we were home. I wanted the cracked broken black tiles of our own bathroom; I wanted our neighbor sitting with me on the front stoop, the smell of the Charles River, our pots without handles and the rickety three-legged couch I complained about every time I sat on it; I wanted normalcy. I said, *Let's make a deal.* Let me win this round and I will never ever again smoke. I will go on great missions and try not to gossip. But more than anything I solemnly swear to never again smoke.

It seemed to take forever, phone calls, a slow walk, the idle chatter and words of sympathy and well wishes from the time-share man, his gaze taking in the freshly raked beach. There was a boat ride, and then an ambulance that really was a station wagon with a light on top. There was an emergency room and then a closed door, a hall where pregnant women perched like hood ornaments on cheap aluminum stretchers, some crying out in labor, their wings spread in pain. They had no ultrasound; they had no answers. I was thinking about the used car lot that was across the street from my grandmother's house when I was growing up. I thought about the little plastic flags strung across that lot and the way they whipped in the wind. *It's a Good Deal* the sign said, and whenever anyone commented on it, my grandmother simply leveled her eyes at the person with a solemn stare, as if to say, you better work hard to *make* it a good deal. I rolled past woman after woman. They looked lifeless; used and worn and tired.

I spent a week sitting in bed or on a chaise on the balcony, the room littered with room service trays; the hotel had limited choices: conch chowder, conch fritters, conch omelet, conch conch. I could hear my husband down below, in my absence forced to hear more time-share news, to have young, supple bodies pointed out for his perusal, while I clicked a channel changer round and round hoping that all of a sudden I would find more than one station. Over and over they advertised a parade that had taken place the week before, people in bird suits, feathers and bells, marching. I lay in the bed and watched little yellow sugar birds fly up to suck the jelly packets I placed outside, the breakfast tray discarded on the dresser. The Kings Day Parade. The Kings Day Parade. It was a bad *Twilight Zone.* It was like the world had stopped suddenly and thrown everything askew.

Everyone has a story. Perfect strangers came up and told me the most horrible story they'd ever heard about pregnancy and childbirth. They would say, "I shouldn't be telling this to *you,*" and then proceed without ever pausing to draw a breath. I heard about the woman who miscarried after the three-month mark and about the woman who knew at seven months that her baby was dead but was asked to carry it into labor all the same. "Oh, sure," people said. "It's common to bleed like that. Happens all the time. No real explanation." Que será será. A miscarriage is just one that was never meant to be, you know, a genetic *mistake.* If you lose this one you can always have another. But look at it this way, you haven't lost it yet! *It ain't over till it's over. The fat lady ain't done singing.*

The river is within us, the sea is all about us. Joseph Sever's voice quavered out the line as he leaned closer to me, all the while looking at my abdomen, now two months beyond the Twilight Zone scare. He insisted that I read aloud, anything I was reading, anything my husband was reading. We should be reading aloud all the time now. He had read an article about it, the words, the sounds traveling through the layers of clothes and skin, thick hard muscle to those miniature ears, lanugo-coated limbs gently swishing and bathing. "Who knows what's for real," Joseph said as he tipped his hat and once again reached for my grocery bag piled high with cigarette substitutes like licorice whips and Chunky Monkey ice cream, greasy Slim-Jim sausage sticks, the taste for which I thought I'd outgrown. "We know nothing of this world, this great universe," he paused, hazel eyes squinting in thought as he waited for me to nod. "Take God, for example," he said and laughed softly, "and which came first, knowledge or man's *need* for knowledge?" I motioned him on with his errand, his own marketing trip. It was our daily struggle, trying to help each other on the icy brick sidewalks. We argued who was more in need: an old man with a bad heart or a pregnant woman who would not believe that everything was really okay until she gave birth to, saw, held, heard a healthy infant.

I dreamed of my grandmother. She was naked and alone in a rubble of upturned graves. I squatted and cradled her in my arms, so happy to find her alive after all, forget the damp orange clay and what seemed like miniature ancient ruins. Forget the pale, shrouded family members wandering aimlessly in search of loved ones. (Was this Judgment Day?) And then I dreamed myself sleeping, my husband on his side, his face a comfort. My own head was inclined toward him. I wore the very gown I wore in reality, and within the dream I woke to a chill, a cool draft that filled the room and I sat, startled, and turned on the lamp by the bed where, stuck to its base, was a little yellow Post-it note with the words, *I came to see if you believe,* written in a small deliberate hand. Yes, yes, I believe. I believe. I woke myself with this affirmation. I woke to discover that my husband was already up and in the shower, and that I wasn't entirely sure to what or to whom I had given this great affirmation of faith. I woke to the tiny buzzsaw, vibrating uterus, a pressed bladder, the dim gray light of day.

Early that summer—week twenty-eight, the time designated for a baby to be "legally viable"—Joseph and I went to see the swans being brought to the Public Garden pond. It was warm and we walked slowly, taking our time to point out to each other lovely panes of amethyst glass, the little catty-corner building that looks just like the drawing in *Make Way for Ducklings,* the bar that was the model for *Cheers,* crowds of people waiting in line to get inside and buy T-shirts.

Joseph talked about how Gwendolyn always saved old bread to scatter for the birds. We sat on a bench in the shadiest spot we could find, the ground in front of us littered with soggy bread that the overfed, fat ducks were ignoring. I told him about the Peabody Hotel in Memphis and how as a child I had been taken there to see the ducks marching from their penthouse to the elevator and down and across the lobby to the pool. I told how I had looked around that lobby and marveled at the people staying there, this fine hotel with its rugs and chandeliers and fountains. I was with a church group, one in a busload of kids stopping here and there to sing for other congregations. It was supposed to be an honor (not to mention an educational experience) to get to go on that trip, but I spent the whole time reading *Richie Rich* comic books and wishing myself home. It was the summer before Martin Luther King was shot. It was when Elvis still walked the rooms of Graceland in the wee hours of the morning. It was when my sister was practicing to be a junior high cheerleader, and my grandmother was still walking the rows of her garden.

With the arrival of the swans (they had been staying across the street at the Ritz), Joseph cleared his throat and began reciting. *Upon the brimming water among the stones are nine and fifty swans.* He paused and laughed, added. "Or what about two swans?" But with Yeats's "wild swans" he had once again opened his favorite topic, which led eventually, as the crowd began to thin—baby strollers pushed away, children led to visit the row of bronze ducklings, couples folding up their picnic blankets—to Eliot and one of his all time favorites, "Journey of the Magi," which led him to "The Gift of the Magi" and then into his own Christmas story, one I'd heard on several other occasions. *Christmas with Gwendolyn.* The picture of Gwendolyn I always conjured up in my mind had the look of a Gibson Girl, even though I knew that she wore her straight gray hair cut close with bangs and that the waist of her dark wool coat hit high around her short, thick middle. He kept a photograph on top of his dresser: Joseph and Gwendolyn in 1945, standing on a busy sidewalk, each cradling a shopping bag, his face filled out in a way I'd never see.

"It was just the two of us," he began as he often did, pausing with the unspoken question—one I never asked—about whether or not they had ever wanted a child. His close attention to my own growth, his comments on my coloring and my hair, seemed answer enough. He described their Christmas Eve, the rushing home from work in the mid-afternoon to find the other waiting on the stoop—her with a black wool scarf wrapped around her head and tied beneath her chin, him with a gray fedora he felt certain she was about to replace that very night. He said that when he looked back it seemed like it always snowed right on cue. *Let there be snow.* Inside, their windows fogged up with the cold, the lights they strung glowed as they pulled old boxes from the closets, tied red velvet around the cats' necks. They waited until dark, and then they walked down to the waterfront, the freezing wind forcing them to walk huddled together like Siamese twins. They listened, ready to stop at the sound of carolers, church bells, paused and looked up into windows to see lights and children and greenery. *The city was never more beautiful.*

They ate in a small dark restaurant at a table by the window. First they ordered bourbons (hers with a lot of water), and then they spent the first hour just talking over the year behind them. Oh, there were those years when the plans went awry, when one or the other was upset about this or that, work or a sick family member; there was that year when, for reasons he didn't feel it necessary to discuss, they were farther apart than they had ever been, complete strangers coming and going for a period of three months. They feared that they would lose each other. That there would be no forgiveness. He said this part quietly, nodded a slight nod as if to say *you must understand what I'm saying.* "That was the worst Christmas," he said quietly. "Really the only bad Christmas." He laughed then and looked at my abdomen, gestured to it as if speaking to the child. "Trust me. We were better people once it was all over. We made it." We watched the swans circling, necks arched proudly as they didn't even acknowledge the various breads and cracker crumbs tossed out onto the water. "In my mind the Christmas, *the* Christmas is the way I've described it. Our dinner, talking over us. Our life and our future."

On all of those Christmas eves, it seemed they were the only people out. Others had rushed home to family gatherings but neither of them had relatives close by. They were alone with each other. The best part of it all was that they always got the very best tree left at the Faneuil Hall lot for just three dollars. (It had gotten up to ten by the time Gwendolyn died.) Then they dragged the tree home and decorated with common little items, things they already had. Paper chains cut from glossy magazine pages, tinfoil stars, spools of thread, her jewelry, his neckties, fishing gear, chess pieces tied off in twine. "We had a glorious time," he said. "Brandy and poetry and her crazy ornaments until the sun, that cold winter light, came through the window."

This Public Garden day, with the temperature at at least eighty as we made our way back down Charles Street, we once again argued over who was in worse shape, a thin old man with a prosthetic heart valve or a pregnant woman so far beyond her normal weight she thought she'd never again wear shoes other than the rubber clogs from Woolworth's. *A hard time we had of it,* he said in short gasps as we began our climb up the dark stairs to our apartments.

I dreamed my husband and I went to a party. We were greeted at the door by the mother of an old friend of mine, a childhood friend I had not seen in years. In real life I knew that the mother had recently died of leukemia, and in the dream I knew this, too. And I knew that it was not my friend's mother who greeted us but a three-dimensional image of her. Somewhere in this room there was a silent projector. My husband said how wonderful she was. He said, *No wonder you love to be over at their house all the time.* (I had not seen the house in twenty years.) I could not bring myself to tell him the truth, that we could pass our hands straight through her body; that there was absolutely nothing there.

The dream jumped the way dreams do, and the party was over; we were almost at the car when I remembered that I had left my coat behind. I raced back only to find an empty room (had the others there been projections as well?) and on the wall was her image, stilled. They were projecting an image I'd forgotten. It wasn't the way she looked, racing up the gold-carpeted stairs of her house, demanding that we explain the cigarette burn in my friend's brand new windbreaker, or the one she wore a year later when she handed me my first sanitary napkin and elastic belt, or the one she wore the day the moving van arrived to take them to California. Rather, the expression I saw, frozen there on the wall of the dream, was one more subtle and fleeting; it was the one she wore most of the time.

My friend and I are in the backseat of her Country Squire. We are taking turns inking the initials of the boys we love (high school boys we've never met) in cryptic fashion on each other's Blue Horse notebooks. In the way back, her brother and his friend are bouncing up and down until her mother casts a quick glance in the rearview mirror. "Settle down, boys," she yells, a forced furrow in her brow. They obey, at least while the light is red, and she goes back to her humming. And this is the moment: the second glance in the rearview mirror, the look after she yells, when her face relaxes into a half smile. On the radio is "We'll Sing in the Sunshine," and she sings along, her voice a little nasal, twangy with confidence. And that's what I see on the wall, over and over, that look, and in that look, I see Indian summer, the fashionable ponchos my friend and I had shed balled up at our feet, the flat terrain of our hometown passing us by.

* * *

I had back labor. We took a taxi across town to the hospital, me stretched and riding as upright as I could manage, my face pressing into the soiled gray ceiling of the cab, smelling the traces of smoke that lingered in the upholstery. The cab was smoke-free, or so the driver said when my husband hailed him; at the time I was squatting in front of our building, my face against the concrete steps. Just the day before, Joseph had been in that very spot waiting for the cab that took him to the very same hospital for a brief stay, a series of routine tests. In the hospital, we were still neighbors, though wings and floors apart, and I wanted to get a message to him but at the moment I felt discombobulated and all tied up. *Would I like narcotics? Why yes, thank you very much.* I said that I'd also appreciate a needle in my spine just as soon as they could round up an anesthesiologist. *Epidural, please.* The words rolled right off my tongue; I had forgotten everything I knew about breathing.

My friend and I were eleven years old and in love with Tommy James and the Shondelles. "Crystal Blue Persuasion" was playing on her little hi-fi on the floor when we heard her mother coming up the stairs.

"Where did you girls get cigarettes?" She flung open the door to my friend's room and stood there, hands on her hips, frosted hair shagged short on top and long on the neck.

"Junior's Texaco," my friend whispered meekly. There was no need to paint the picture, the two of us riding double on her banana-seat bike, me pedaling furiously while she held on to my waist, her legs held stiffly out from the spokes. We were on the service road of the interstate. The glittering black asphalt was still steaming from a recent rain.

Labor went on forever. A monitor was strapped to my belly for contractions, another to the baby's head for its pulse. I was telling jokes and calling my sister long distance by then. I was watching a contraction rise like an earthquake reading, the needle going wild to register my unfelt pain. I was ready to push when I realized that I'd been talking for hours and that the doctor had never left my side. Then I realized that all was not well, that my husband was too quiet. I had come this far—no cigarette had come close to my mouth—and yet, there was a problem. The baby's heart rate dropped, a heart so small I couldn't even imagine. It was a simple procedure, this C-section, but it had to be done quickly, now, this instant. They knew what to do; they had all of the right equipment to slice through the layers of skin and muscle, to pluck from my body a fully formed baby.

JILL McCORKLE

My friend's mother reached into her bathroom cabinet and handed me a sanitary napkin and a little elastic belt. I had seen them before. I had practiced wearing one at home; I had envied those girls who had already turned the monumental corner. She said that she understood if I felt I needed to go home, but she really hoped that I'd stay the night as we had planned. I stood bare-footed on the cool tile floor of her bathroom, my eyes still red from chlorine, my hair bleached and like straw from the local pool. I watched the toilet paper and the fancy little embroidered guest towels sway with the blast of central air conditioning. She sat on the end of her bed, the first queen-size I ever saw, and talked while I nodded embarrassedly. Here was the moment I had been waiting for, the threshold, and I felt gawky and foolish and uncomfortable. But I stayed, and we went to Teen Night at the community pool, where we played Ping-Pong and sat on the hard wooden benches that lined the chain link fenced area. I felt like I was sitting on a garden hose but maintained my position for fear that the outline would be seen through my shorts. I kept thinking about my friend's mother on the foot of that bed, ankles crossed, a flash of pale pink polish on her toenails. A million years later, when I heard about a girl several years older who faked sick to stay home from school and then slept with her boyfriend in her parents' house, this was the bedroom I pictured, even though they had long since moved to California. I saw the bed, the chenille spread pulled up tight, pillows rolled and pressed against the scratched headboard. I saw the brown tiles of her bathroom floor, smelled the blast of central air and the lingering chlorine. My friend's sixth-grade school picture was on the dresser in a heavy gold frame. At the height of first love, Saturday nights in parked cars or on the busted couch of somebody's forsaken game room, the friction of adolescent passion driving me forward, I thought of that picture; the bed, the coolness, the distant glance, all insecurities and reservations temporarily brushed aside.

The day after my daughter was born, I woke to great relief, which was quickly followed by a fit of anger, a cold apprehension of what might have been or might not have been. Fifty years ago and maybe my child and I would have been the names with young ages on tombstones. Many times I had gone with my mother and grandmother to tend my grandfather's grave; they weeded and planted, brushed the pine needles from his marble footmarker. My grandmother pushed a whirring handmower up and down the hill of his plot. I never knew him, her husband, my mother's father, my grandfather, but I imagined him stretched out there beneath the dirt; I saw a young man in a World War One uniform even though I know he lived to be a very different man, a much older, frailer man, with wiry gray hair. On a nearby grave there was a tiny stone lamb and dates that equaled nothing, the baby born and died on the same day, the mother dead just one day later. The more I looked over the mossy slabs, the more I found. "Oh honey," my grandmother said and squeezed my hand. "It *is* sad." So many of them must have died for such simple, simple reasons.

I asked that the stitches in my abdomen be eternally blessed; I praised modern medicine, saluted and sang. I called everyone I knew or had heard about who had, in so many words, squatted out in the woods like an animal, gnawed tree bark and umbilical cord, stoically delivered in absolute isolation. "You idiot. You goddamned selfish idiot," I raged and hung up before they knew who I was. In some places I am thought to have an accent.

Hurricane Andrew took the hotel in the Virgin Islands and all of the nearby time shares. I keep thinking of the place as if it still exists. I do the same with Joseph Sever. We moved a year after my daughter was born, and when we left, an August day much like the one of our arrival, he was out on the stoop wearing his panama hat and reading the *Boston Globe*.

The week before the move, we had finally done all of those things that visitors do: the bus tour, the battleship, the Old North Church. I spent a whole afternoon at the top of the Prudential building, my daughter tucked away in the little sack I wore strapped to my chest, as I fed quarter after quarter into the viewfinders. In a random glance toward Beacon Hill, I spotted the steeple of the church on our street, and from there it was easy to swing back and find our building, to travel up the red brick to the roofline. I found our bay window, the plant on the sill; I half expected to see myself enter the room, my abdomen round and hard and waiting. I had that same odd feeling that I get from time to time, the feeling that maybe I *can* pick up the phone and call my childhood friend or my grandmother at those memorized numbers long disconnected. That I can find a clean path into my childhood where I might race my bike, down the street and into the yard, the wheels spinning and clicking—a triangle cut from an aluminum pie pan clothes-pinned to a spoke. That I *can* run inside and find my parents, thirty years younger, younger than I am now, as they talk over some event that will soon be lost to that hour. I moved the lens just one hundredth of an inch, and there was Joseph's living room, the outline of what might have been a cat.

We exchanged greetings over the next couple of years—Christmas cards, postcards. The last card to arrive was addressed to my daughter, an Easter card, one of those you open and confetti comes out. I hate those drop-what-you're-doing-and-go-get-the-Dustbuster cards, and yet there I was, my daughter delighted by the sparkled shapes, while I imagined him there on Charles Street in one of the fancy card stores, thumbing through racks in search of the right one. The news that he died came from another neighbor in the building, and even then, seeing it all in print, it didn't seem quite real. I couldn't imagine the orphaned cats being given away or the years' worth of warped books pulled from the kitchen cupboard, the dilapidated bedside lamp left on the curb in a heap of garbage bags along with *The Heart of Darkness* and all the makings of a thrown-together Christmas. Instead I saw, see, him out on the stoop or down at the corner grocery picking his fruit from a table out front, his breath visible and keeping time with the click of his heart.

My friend and I went to the cemetery to smoke cigarettes. She pedaled the bike that time. Her legs weren't as strong as mine, so we wobbled and nearly fell on the small dirt paths. It was a new cemetery, the kind where there are no raised stones, only flat slates of marble at the foot of each grave. The flowers, whether artificial or real, looked as if they had sprung up from the graves. People in our town liked the smooth new look and the serene white statue of Jesus in the center. But as I inhaled and exhaled, narrowed my eyes like I'd seen smokers do, I told my friend that I preferred the place my grandfather was buried. I liked the huge trees, perfect for tire swings and clubhouses, except they were in a cemetery. I liked the moss and the dates before I was born. Here, the people had started dying in the sixties, and it all seemed too close. I told my friend how my dad could palm a lit Camel nonfilter and hide it in his pants, how he had once done that in high school when the principal walked by. I had heard the story many times, and I had seen enough old photos to picture him there, his hair combed back high off his forehead—a pompadour—as he leaned, tall and thin, against the brick wall of the gymnasium. I turned my cigarette inward, heat near my hand, to demonstrate. My friend did the same, the fabric of her jacket singeing when she tried to slide her hand into her pocket. We smoked and smoked until our heads felt light, and then we each chewed three pieces of Teaberry gum and rubbed our hands in the yellow clay of a grave recently dug. Everywhere else there was perfect green grass, rolled out like a carpet, flowers sprouting up from the dead.

I think of that place every autumn when I kneel to plant bulbs, when I sprinkle a teaspoon of bonemeal into each hole, as my grandmother advised. And at Christmas I pull up Joseph's scene, the walk to buy the tree, the brandy and makeshift adornments. I give Gwendolyn Gibson Girl hair and a rhinestone cigarette holder. I give her the face of my friend's mother. "How old will you be when I'm one hundred?" my daughter asks, enunciating in a way I will never master, and I say, "One hundred and thirty one." I catch myself looking at her in absolute amazement, that she is here and the time is now. A faster sperm and she wouldn't be here; there would be another child or no child at all. No day beyond that moment would be exactly as I know it now. It might not be a bad life, just a different one. What we don't know is enormous. "I want you to live forever," she tells me. "I want a guinea pig and a Fantastic Flower kit. I want long wavy hair, and I want to be like Jesus and have people pray to the god of me forever." I tell her that I would like nothing better, that it's every young mother's dream.

* * *

Sometimes I think of the woman, cheered by the long-awaited phone call that she is pregnant. The nurse on the other end is relieved. Everyone is overjoyed. She goes upstairs to take a nap and never wakes, an ectopic hemorrhage. Would the fanatics in the street argue that the life within, this bundle of cells unintelligible to the human eye, killed *her,* these people who rummage the back-alley dumpsters of emergency rooms to find some hideous example of sin in a jar, these people who take someone else's worldly loss and turn it into a freak show? I can barely keep my car on the road when I see them gathered in protest, their hideous pictures waving in the air. "Why don't you *get* a life?" I want to yell. "Go after handguns. Go after R. J. Reynolds."

I dreamed of my grandmother; I lifted her as she had once lifted me, my feet potty-black from her garden, through the damp, dirt-floored shed where she stored her jars of tomatoes and peaches, floating jewels, pickled and preserved. In the dream I watched people wandering, stones overturned, granite lambs tilted on the heaving mounds of cracked earth. Was this Judgment Day? "I don't know what all the fuss is about," she said, and I was there holding her pulling her closer, corn and tobacco fields beyond the upturned graves, holding her, and whispering the song she made up years before, a lullaby sung to the tune of an unknown hymn, *you're my baby, you're my baby, you're my baby, yes, you are.*

When I was fifteen, I spent many afternoons cruising the streets of my hometown with a friend who drove a baby-blue Mustang. It was a car to be envied, and we were like queens, the radio blasting the top forty, our suntanned arms hung out the window to flick our cigarettes. I was a bonafide smoker then, a pack of Salems in the zippered part of my vinyl purse, fifty cents in my pocket in case I ran out. Sometimes we drove way out of the city limits, out where we were surrounded by flat fields and little wood-framed houses, churchyards overgrown, the rush of the brisk country air drowning out the music of the radio. Those rides gave me such a rush, tingling scalp and racing heart; I felt powerful, like I could look out over those fields to the end of the world.

Now I find my daughter all dressed up in front of a mirror. She is almost five and is wearing a faux-leopard poncho and a little pillbox hat with netting over her face. Her high heels are silver sequined and wobbling to one side. She has a pencil held between two fingers and with her other hand on her hip, takes a deep drag from the imaginary cigarette. She tilts her head back, purses her lips and blows at her image, eyes closed while she says, "I must be running now, my dear." She turns quickly and stops when she sees me there, her shoes leaving marks as if she had suddenly put on brakes. "Oh, hello," she says in the same affected tone. "I'm pretending it's long, long ago. Back when cigarettes were good for you." With that she takes another puff and blows her smoke my way, and I lean close to breathe it all in. I breathe in as much as I can take for now.

PART II

Final Vinyl Days

I'll never forget the day Betts moved in. How could I? Open the apartment door, and there she is, with two suitcases, a purple futon, and two milk crates full of albums.

It was 1984, the day after Marvin Gaye died. That's how I remember so well. I had just gotten home from my job at Any Old Way You Choose It Music, where the Marvin Gaye bin had emptied within a couple of hours. I'd spent the afternoon marveling at what happens when somebody kicks. Marvin's bin, other than for the Motown faithfuls and a brief flurry after *The Big Chill,* was long neglected; I had even *dusted* it back when everybody was BeeGee Disco Crap berserk. Now Marvin is dead, and there's a run on his music. I had watched the same thing happen with Elvis and John Lennon, always good sellers, but incredibly so when they died.

"You want me here don't you?" Betts asked. Her thick, dark hair was to her shoulders, and her eyes were wide open, always as if she were seeing the world for the first time, like every object caught her attention. She stared at me; I was the object of her attention for the moment. "I mean I've been staying here every night, so I might as well have my things, right? And by the way," she was saying, "I could use some help." The purple futon was unrolled and already halfway inside the apartment. "We don't need this, but Helen said she didn't want it." Helen, the roommate, was a physics major who liked to test all the physical properties during sex. Betts had said (before she started coming to my place) that it was driving her crazy (the shaking plaster and peculiar sounds). I didn't tell her, but it was driving *me* crazy, for different reasons, the main one being that I was a wee bit curious about what took place on the other side of the wall that separated Bett's room from Helen's. Bett's side was pretty tame: a bulletin board covered in little notes and photos and ticket stubs, a huge poster of a skeleton. She was majoring in physical therapy and was taking it all seriously (too seriously if you ask me), or depending, *not* seriously enough. "I am not a masseuse," she said often enough with no smile whatsoever. Short on sense of humor but long on legs. Sometimes you buy an album for just one song, thinking that the others will start to grow on you. When she finally got the futon in, she dug out her Duran Duran album, and that's when I drew the line. We were from different time zones. She had a whole list of favorite *good old songs*: "Afternoon Delight" and "Muskrat Love" were two.

I played Marvin: "Stubborn Kind of Fella," "It Takes Two," "Mercy Mercy Me." She just shrugged and went back in my room to arrange her little junk on the top of my dresser and the back of the commode. I sat there with Marvin, tried to imagine what it must feel like to know that your old man is about to kill you like Marvin did.

Why did he wear that hat all the time?" Betts asked looking the same way she did when she asked me why I still wore my hair long enough to pull back in a ponytail. "Is he the guy who sings that 'Sexual Healing' song?" She was standing in the kitchen with a two-liter Diet Coke in one hand and a handful of Chee-tos in the other. She's a healthy one. She bitches about an occasional joint. It's okay for her to go downtown and pound down beer with her girlfriends, but for God's sakes don't do anything illegal in moderation. "We've got to fix this place," she was saying. "And did you say you were going back to graduate school in the fall?"

"No." I shook my head. She was peeking under a dishcloth like she expected a six-foot snake under there. She sounded like my mother, asking me if I said what she knows I never in the hell did. Those were her words, *graduate school.* When my mom does it, the secret words are *electrical appliance store.* My old man owns one in a town so big it actually has two gas stations, and he'd rather pull his nose off of his face with a wrench or beat up a new Maytag washer than to have me in his employment. Mom says things like, "Didn't you say you were looking for a job where you can advance in the business?" That's when I always click the phone up and down or flip on the blender and plead bad connection. It's a real bad connection, Mom.

And there stood Betts, swigging her Nutrasweet, eating her fluorescent cheese, waiting for an answer.

"You know that night we first met, you said you had been in law school and were thinking about going back."

"I said that?" I asked.

She nodded.

"Did I tell you I quit law school and joined VISTA?

Spent a year in the Appalachian mountains with diarrhea?"

She nodded a bored affirmative.

"Did I tell you I loved it?"

"No."

"Well, that's because I didn't. But what I learned in that year is that I could do anything I wanted to do, you know?"

"So?" She took a big swallow of her nutrasyrup, then wiped her mouth and hands with enough paper towels to equal a small redwood. "What are you going to do?"

"I'm doing it." I lifted the stylus off of Marvin and cleaned the album, my hand steady as I watched the Motown label spin. She was still staring in disbelief. A real bad connection. As good looking as she was, it was a real bad connection. I left for five minutes, long enough to go pee and see her little ceramic eggs filled with perfumed cedar shavings on the back of the john, and in that five minutes, she put on Boy George. What we prided ourselves on most at Any Old Way You Choose It Music then was that we did just that, *chose it* without regard to what sells and top tens and who's who. Like if I was in one mood, I might play the Beatles all day long, might play "Rubber Soul" two times in a row. I had whole weekends where all I played were the Stones, Dylan, or the Doors and then followed it with a

Motown Monday, a Woodstock Wednesday. Some days I just went for somebody like Buffy St. Marie or Joan Baez, which surprised the younger clientele, people like Betts, people who might say, who's that? Screw them.

"You mean you're going to work there forever?" Betts asked. Boy George stared up at me from the floor. Bett's fingers were tapping along to "Do You Really Want to Hurt Me?"

"I'm buying in," I told her, which was not entirely a lie. The owner, a guy my age who had already made it big in the local business scene, was considering it. He graduated with a D average from a second-rate junior college and received a small empire already carved out by his old man. I graduated from the university with a 3.7 in English and philosophy, highest honors for some old paper I wrote about Samuel Coleridge, and what I got was one of those leather kits for your toiletries. *What toiletries?* I had wanted to ask my mom, who told me she remembered me saying I needed one of those. Yeah, right. I *need* a toiletries kit.

"I'm doing okay," I said and lifted the stylus from Boy George, searched in earnest for the Kinks so Betts could ask some more dumb questions. She came over and knelt beside me, put her head close to mine, little orange Cheeto sparkles above her lip.

"I know you're doing okay," she whispered and pressed her mouth against my neck. "You're better than okay," she said. "My friends all think you're interesting in a kind of weird way, you know, mysterious."

Her own anatomy was doing quite nicely. Too nicely really, because it was making me a dishonest person. I was thinking *bad connection, bad connection,* while I let her play her albums and pull me to the floor.

"Isn't it great I've moved in?" she asked ten minutes later as the needle hugged the wide smooth grooves of the last song, a long and silent begging to be lifted.

"Isn't it going to be wonderful?" she asked.

But all I could think about when I closed my eyes was Marvin standing there in his hat, his old man with pistol aimed.

Betts moved in the day after he died. He hadn't been dead three months when she moved out. She pled guilty to not *truly* loving me, and I turned on the somber broken-hearted look long enough to pack up her books and hand them out to the squat-bodied pathology resident she'd taken up with and who was waiting for her. "Here's a live one for you," I told him and patted her on the back.

* * *

I didn't miss *her* so much as I just missed. The jerky young store owner was still dangling his carrot about *maybe* letting me buy in. I told him he was getting too far away from the old stuff, the good stuff, but he insisted that we go *with the flow*. He didn't want me monopolizing the sound system with too much of the old stuff; he said Neil Young made his skin crawl. He was sick over the fact that he hadn't kept the Rick Nelson stock up to date. I figured what the hell, did I *really* want to be in business with such a sleaze? I took a little vacation to get myself feeling up, to get Betts out of my bones, and then I was back full force, nothing on the back of my john, no album that never should have been on my shelves in the first place. But before too long, there I was hanging up T-shirts of the Butthole Surfers. Things were getting bad.

I thought they couldn't get any worse, but I let a couple of years spin by and they did. There were prepubescent girls with jewelry store names running around shopping malls singing songs they didn't deserve to sing. It was plagiarism; it was distasteful. Where were the *real* women? Where was Grace Slick? Then there was a run on Roy Orbison's music, and once again my jerk of a boss was in a state of panic that he'd missed yet another good-time oldie postmortem sale. He was eating cocaine for breakfast by then and had a bad case of the DBCs (Dead Brain

Cells). I might sleep around now and then; I might even end up with somebody who was born after 1968, but at least I'm moral about it. He gets them tanked and snorted and then goes for the prize. One step above being a necro if you ask me. And what really pisses me off is that society sees me as the loser, the social misfit who's living in the past. The guy drives a BMW and owns a condo and a business, stuffs all his money up his nose, pokes teenage coeds who don't remember that he did it. And he's successful.

I was about to the point where I couldn't tune it all out, when I wound up with a bad hangover that turned into the flu and landed me in one of those fast-food medicine places. You know, a Doc in the Box, planted right beside Revco so you can rush over and fill your prescriptions. I felt like hell, and I was about to stretch out on their green vinyl couch and snooze, when I saw someone familiar. It was Marlene Adams, a girl from home, a woman of my time, no ring on her hand, good-looking as ever. I sat straight up and was about to say something when she turned calmly and called my name. "I was wondering when you'd recognize me," she said and laughed, her eyes as blue as the crisp autumn sky. "I had heard you were still living around here. Who told me that? Somebody I saw at a wedding not too long ago." For a split second I was feeling better, like grabbing a bucket of chicken and sitting in the park, throwing a Frisbee, going to some open-air concert.

"You haven't changed a bit," she said, and I felt her gaze from head to toe. It was the first time in years that I was *worried* about how I looked. "Neither have you." I sat up straight, smoothed back my hair. God, why hadn't I taken a shower? "Why're you here?" I asked and glanced to the side where there was a cloudy aquarium with one goldfish swimming around. "I thought you were some place like California or Colorado or North Dakota. I thought you were married." I thought that fish must feel like the only son of a bitch on the planet, thirty gallons of water and nobody to swim over and talk to.

"Divorced. I'm back in graduate school, psychology," she said and laughed. "And I'm in this office because I fell down some steps." I turned back from the dismal fish to see her holding out her right foot. Her ankle was blue and swollen. She had on a little white sock, the kind my mother always wore with her tennis shoes, with little colored pom-pom balls hanging off the backs.

"Can you believe it?" She shook her head back and forth. "It was really embarrassing. There were loads of people in the library when it happened." She leaned back, her thick hair fanning behind her as she stared up at the ceiling. I kept expecting her to say something really stupid and mundane and patronizing like *So, you say that you're living here but not in graduate school, you sell albums and tapes to coeds you occasionally sleep with, you say that you have a hangover, what I'm hearing from you is that you are in search of a sex partner who has possibly heard some songs from your youth.*

"I'm just as clumsy as I was the time we went camping," she said, her voice light and far removed from the monotone I'd just imagined. "Remember? You swore you'd never take me again?"

"And I didn't," I said. "I never got the chance." I turned back to the fish. It was an awkward moment. You don't often get to discuss breaking up years after the fact, but we were doing it. She dumped me, and now that I had reminded her of that fact, she was talking in high gear to cover the tracks. *Why does it take so long to get seen in this place?* and *Do you ever get home? Does your dad still have the refrigerator store and is your mom well?*

I was relieved when the door opened and the nurse called me in. "See you around," I said politely, half hoping that she'd disappear while I was gone. Marlene and I were the same age, from the same small town, the same neighborhood, even. I had known her since my family moved there when I was in the fifth grade and we had all run around screaming the words to "I Want to Hold Your

Hand" while making faces and crossing our eyes like Ringo did. Our common ground and memories was what had brought us together that month in college to begin with.

I thought about it while they stuck a thermometer in my mouth and instructed me to undress. Marlene had been pretty goofy as a kid, and though I considered her a friend, I never would have ridden my bike over to her house to *visit*. She had this dog named Alfie who smelled like crap, which left Marlene and her wet-dog-smelling jeans rather undesirable. In junior high, Matt Walker and I had suggested we put Alfie in front of a firing squad, and Marlene didn't speak to me for weeks after. No big deal, but then in high school we got to be pals just sort of hanging outside in the breezeway where you were allowed to smoke in between classes. Can you believe they *let* us smoke at school? That *they,* the administrators, those lopsided adults had *designated* an area? I spent a lot of time there, and so did Marlene. She was on the Student Council, which most of us thought was a bunch of crap. She was forever circulating some kind of petition. She was really into womanhood, which I found kind of titillating in a strange way, don't ask me why, though I never did anything about it at the time. She was a hard worker, a smart girl. That's the kind of shit people wrote in her yearbook if they wrote anything at all. Nineteen seventy was not a big year for yearbook signing. But then, get the girl off to college, and there is major metamorphosis. It was like I could watch it happening there in a poli sci lecture, blond streaks in her hair that hung to her waist, little shortie T-shirts and cutoff jeans, her tinted wire-rim glasses (aviator style, like Gloria Steinem) always pushed up on her head. Guys waited to see where she was going to sit and then clustered around her. God, she was beautiful, and then I had to take a turn just sitting and *listening* to all that was going on in her life, just as she had *listened* to me there in the smoking area. I had a girlfriend here and there along the way, but I guess I was really waiting for Marlene to come around. Her boyfriend had been drafted, and though she told me how lucky I was not to have been taken (lucky break, legal blindness; my brother winged me with a sharp rock when I was seven), I could tell that I was weakened in her eyes. There would have been much more admiration had I had twenty-twenty vision and fled to Canada. It was a brief affair, the consummation of any likes we'd had for each other since adolescence, and then it was over, one fiasco of a camping trip, pouring down rain, Marlene spraining her thumb when she tripped over a tree limb and landed face down in the mud. It amazed me the things that that damn thumb *hindered* her from doing. It was a loss of a weekend.

"You have the flu," the nurse told me after I'd waited forever in my underwear, and I made my way back out to the lone-fish lobby to find her still there, though now her ankle was all neatly bound in an Ace bandage.

"You don't look so great," she said. "Why don't I go home with you and fix you something for lunch." I shrugged, thinking about what was in my kitchen cabinet, a moldy loaf of bread, a couple of cans of tomato soup, one can of tuna. If she could turn it into something, I'd beg her never to leave me.

"What about your car?" I asked. Again she pointed to her ankle.

"I can't drive. My ankle." For a minute she sounded just like she had years before, *I can't do that, my thumb,* and I should have listened to the warning, but I was too taken by her features, a face that needed no makeup of any kind, a girl who *looked* like she *ought* to be a perfect camper.

"I rode the bus here," she said and extended her hand for me to help her up. "It'll be fun to catch up on things."

Marlene and I picked up with each other like we'd never been apart. It was like we could read each other's mind, and so we carefully avoided talking about the time we broke up. Instead we focused on all the good times, things we had in common just by being the same age and from the same town. Like I might say, "Remember when Tim Oates cut off the tip of his finger in shop?" and she'd say, "Yeah, he was making a TV table for his mama." Things like that. We had things in common that might *seem* absolutely stupid to an outsider. After three glorious months—triple our first time together— Marlene and I finally got around to talking about all the things that ruined us before. She was starting to kind of hint about how she was going to be a professional, and how maybe I would want to be *a professional,* too. I sang her that song, "I see by your outfit that you are a cowboy, you see by my outfit that I'm a cowboy, too."

"C'mon," she said and wrapped her arms around my neck, "I don't mean to give you a hard time, it's just I've heard you say how you really want . . ."

Bad connection, bad connection. "So get you an outfit and let's all be cowboys." I finished the song, and she went to take her exam in a huff. I did what I always do when I'm feeling lousy, which is to sort through my albums and play all of my favorite cuts. I should have been a deejay, the lone jockey on the late-night waves, rather than employee to a squat coked-to-the-gills little rich shit. I thought of Marlene writing some spiel about *composure:* heal thyself. I was playing Ten Years After full blast, Sly and the Family Stone on deck. And then all in one second I felt mad as hell, as mad as I'd been on that pouring-rain camping trip when Marlene told me that it was hard for her to think of me as anything except *a friend*. She actually said that. It all came back to me when I saw that old Black Sabbath album, which is what she had left behind that other time she moved out. Thanks a whole helluva lot. Warms my heart to see a green-faced chick draped in scarves wandering around what looks like a mausoleum. She had said *all* the routine things you can think of to say. "I know you don't really care about me," she had said. "I could be *anybody*."

"Yeah, right," I had told her. "I could cuddle up with Pat Paulsen and not care. I'm just that kind of insensitive jerk."

"But you don't care about *me*," she had said and pounded her chest with her hand, which was wrapped in a bath towel to protect the sprained thumb that had left her an absolute invalid. "I need to be my own person, have my own life."

I found out a day later that she already had all the info on those schools in the West; she had been looking for a good time to bail out, and it seemed camping out in a monsoon was perfect. It was hard to remember, but it seemed I said something like, "And I don't need to have my own life?" and then the insults got thicker until before long I was told that I was apathetic and chauvinistic and my brain was stuck between my legs.

"So that's why you're always asking what I'm thinking," I said in response. By that time we were soaking wet and driving back *down* the rest of this mountain in the piece-of-crap car I had at the time, an orange Pinto, with a Jimi Hendrix tape playing full blast (eight-track of course). "And what kind of stupid question is that anyway, but you always ask it. *What are you thinking?*" Yeah, that was how the whole ride home went, and of course any time I had a good line, any time I scored, she got to cry and say what an ass I was.

By the time she got home from her lousy test, I was as mad as if I were still there in the pouring rain, jacking that screwed-up Pinto to change a flat while she sat in the passenger side and stared straight ahead at the long stretch of road we had to travel before I could put her out. Apparently, she had been thinking it through as well, because she walked into my apartment looking just as she had when I dumped her out in front of her dorm years before. We had both played over the old stuff enough that we had independently been furious and now were simply exhausted and ready to have it all end, admit the truth.

Nothing in common other than walking the planet at the same time. She was barely over her divorce, she rationalized (he had dumped her I was delighted to find). I handed her that Black Sabbath album on her way out for the second time, and we made polite promises about keeping in touch.

And now I've come to this: Final Vinyl Days, the end of an era. Perfectly round black vinyl discs sit inside their faded jackets on the small table in front of my checkout and await extinction. I stare across the street, the black asphalt made shiny by the drizzling rain, the traffic light blinking red and green puddles in the gray light where a mammoth parking deck is under construction. There I see the lights in the store we compete with, Record City, and I can't help but wonder when they'll change their name; CD Metropolis. But what can I say about names? Any Old Way You Choose It ain't exactly true either.

"Record City doesn't have *these,*" my boss had said just last week and began sticking this crap up all over the place. You know, life-size cutouts of Marilyn Monroe and Elvis, miniature replicas of the old tabletop jukeboxes that are *really* CD houses, piñatas, and big plastic blow-up dinosaurs. I work nights now, not as much business, and I don't have to argue with the owner about what I play overhead. As far as I'm concerned, the new kids on the block are still Bruce Springsteen and Jackson Browne. My boss said it was a promotion, but I know better. Janis Joplin's singing now, "Me and Bobby McGee." And the Stones are on deck with "Jumping Jack Flash." The Stones are the cockroaches of rock. They'll be around when civilization starts over, and I cling to this bit of optimism.

I had no choice but to give in to CDs. And yeah, they sound great, that's true. It's just the principle of the thing, your hand forced to change. Not to even mention the dreaded task of *replacing*. It's impossible. Think of what's *not* available. I'm just taking my time is all. I figure if I just go from the year of my birth to the year I graduated from college, it'll take the rest of my life. I'm going alphabetically so that I don't miss anything and it's a bored, calculated way to approach life. I mean, what if that's how I dealt with women. Imagine it: Betts, Erica, Gail, Marlene, Nancy, that one who always wore black—either Pat or Pam—Susie, Xanadu. Yeah, right, Xanadu. I thought it was kinda cute that she had gone and renamed herself. Then I learned that she had never even heard of Coleridge. Hers was some vivid childhood memory of Olivia Newton John. Scary. We were in a bar, and it was very very late so what could I expect? "Let's get physical," I suggested, and she raised her pencil-thin eyebrows as if trying to remember where she'd heard *that* line before. "Can I call you Xan?"

"Oh, sure," she said, "everybody does." And when she walked ahead of me to the door, I noticed her spiderweb stockings complete with rhinestone spider. She wore a very tight black miniskirt, and I realized that my knowledge of women's fashions had come full circle. I looked at myself in the beer-can-lined mirror to affirm that, yes, I had hit bottom. Xan and I had *nothing* in common except cotton mouth and body hair.

Now Del Shannon has gone and shot himself, and no one has even *asked* about his music. I hear the song "Runaway" and I see myself, a typical nine-year-old slouch, stretched out on my bed with a stack of comic books and the plug of my transistor radio wedged in my ear. My mom made me a bedspread that looked like a race car. The headlights down at the end faced into the hallway where my dad was standing in his undershirt, his face coated in lather. "C'mon, honey," my mom said. "We've got to get down to the store," and then there we all were in front of this little cinder-block store at the edge of town, our last name painted in big red letters on the window. There must have been at least ten people gathered for the opening, an event my dad later said (while we waited for our foot-long hot dogs to be delivered to the window of the car) was just about the proudest moment of his life. He said it was second only to marrying my mother (she had vanilla shake on her lips as she smiled back at him) and having my younger brother and me. My brother was in a French-fry frenzy, bathing the fries in the pool of catsup he'd poured into the cardboard container, but he stopped to take in the seriousness of my dad's announcement. I remember wondering how you *know* when it's the happiest moment and being dumbfounded that anyone could build a life on refigerators and stoves and be happy about it. It amazes me to think that I ever sat in the backseat of that old Chevrolet and looked at my parents (younger then than I am now) and thought how ridiculously *outdated* they were.

Now this coed comes in. Tie-dye is *back*, torn jeans, leather sandals. If her hair wasn't purple and aimed at the ceiling, I could just about console my grief. "Can I help?" I ask, totally unprepared for the high squeak of a voice that comes out. She sounds like she just inhaled a balloon full of helium.

"I want *The Little Mermaid,*" she says. She is wearing a high school ring on her finger. "You know, the video? It's for my little brother."

"Yeah, right. Over there." I point to the far wall, the latest addition to any record/CD/video store, a menagerie of colorful piñatas swinging overhead. "We got 'em all."

Oh, yeah. We've got a two-foot table boasting the end of my youth, leftover albums, the bottom of the barrel. It's all that's left and nobody stops to look, to mourn, to pay respect. I arranged them such that Joni Mitchell is the one looking out on the dreary day. I imagine someone coming in from the street and saying, "Oh, I get it, *paved paradise and put up a parking lot,*" but no such luck; there is no joy in Mudville.

I try to make myself feel better. I think of the positive factors in my life. I recycle my cans and glass and paper. I ride a bike instead of driving a car. Though my old man and I don't see eye to eye, I know that I'll never turn to find him with a gun pointed my way like Mr. Gaye did to Marvin. I sleep peacefully, all bills paid, no TV blasting MTV like the one across the street in the cinder-block house where a couple of girls come and go. One of them is nice-looking in a kind of Marlene way, wears gym clothes all the time, no makeup, hair long and loose. Though I know sure as hell if I slept with her she'd get up and put on lipstick and control-top pantyhose and ask me why I don't cut my hair and get a real job. It's the luck of the draw, and my luck is lousy. "Give up the Diet Coke," I had told Betts. "Give up the fluorescent foods." I had told Marlene to give up the self-pity; if she wanted to be somebody, then to stop talking about it and be it. I had suggested to Xan that she give up the body hair. I told the boss to be *different,* not to cave in to all this new crap. The bottom line? Nobody likes suggestions. So why am I supposed to be different?

"What can you tell me about the Byrds?"

My heart leaps up and I turn to face the purple-haired squeaky-voiced girl who has placed *The Little Mermaid* on the counter and has a twenty clutched in her fist.

"Yeah? The Byrds? Like 'turn, turn, turn?'"

She looks around, first one way then the other. Then she looks back at me, face young and smooth and absolutely blank. "The pink ones," she squeaks and points upward where flamingo piñatas swing on an invisible cord. "How much?"

I watch her walk off now, her pilgrim shoes mud splattered as she heads through the construction area, her pink bird clutched to her chest along with *The Little Mermaid.* It's times like this when I start thinking I might give my dad a call and say, "I know you've been saying how you want me to take over your business some day. . . ." It's times like this when I start thinking about Marlene, when I start forgetting how bad it all got. I do crazy things like start to imagine us meeting again, one more try at this perfect 1970 romance. Like maybe I *will* go to work for my dad, and in my off-hours maybe I'll get out the old power saw and make my mom a TV table (just like you've been saying you wanted, Mom), and maybe I'll circumcise the old index finger and end up in the emergency room, and I'll look down a row of plastic chairs and there she'll be. It's not the *perfect* fantasy, but it's one I have. It's one that more and more starts looking good after I watch Marvin's music revived by a bunch of fat raisins dancing around on the tube, or after I see a series of younger and younger women arriving at my door in their spider hose and stiff neon hair, their arms filled with little plastic squares, a mountain of CD covers dumped on my floor.

Dysfunction 101

My friend Mary Edna goes out every night of the week. She has a few drinks and then dances until they close the door of Roy's Holiday Lounge. It's on I-95, so she's forever meeting folks passing through town. One day she dances with somebody from Dixon, Illinois, and then it's Richmond, Virginia, and of course she has a steady batch from the army base just an hour away. Once she met somebody from Saudi Arabia (she said *Saudia* Arabia), and she talked about that for weeks, as if touching his dark hairy hands (her description) had linked her to lands and histories unknown, like he might be an oil sheik and come a calling again. Lord. She wears their towns like badges, remembers them better by the sorts of details that a tourist might remember than she does hair or eye color (she does always provide that information as well, though it's clear after years of this that she is not a choosy woman). I suggested once, in a moment of sarcasm, that she get one of those big maps and start sticking pins in it, like all those richer-than-thou folks who have in mind seeing every square inch of the planet. I said, "You can get different colored pin heads—fast dancer, slow dancer, smoker, joker, poker, toker, and any of the above." She claims that the only time she ever slept with one of her late-night acquaintances was with the one with cancer who had never had oral sex. It was on his list of things to do on earth —it was right under "see the Grand Canyon" and right above "eat snails and frogs in a French diner." She sure can pick them.

I have tried on many occasions to adopt Mary Edna's children; I feel I might as well, since all those nights their mama is out playing around, they are here at my house taking bubble baths and doing their homework. They stare at me with round brown eyes while we sit around my kitchen table, all three of us in footie pajamas. I rent movies like *Thomasina* and *The Parent Trap* and *Old Yeller,* and we eat big bowls of ice cream with Hershey's syrup, just like I did when I was a kid—like I did with Mary Edna beside me in the house on Fourth Street, my grandmama's house. I thought the two of us would grow up to catch the world by its tail like a comet, and now I look at us and wonder what on earth happened. I told her just the other day that this was what I was wondering, and she asked, who did I think we were, those idiots who committed suicide in hopes of riding a comet? I realized right then that we did not have the same memories and never would. We were two girls with so much in common, and yet we had walked away with such different messages; hers was find a man, any man, and mine was find a decent man—a kind, smart, hard-working, loving man, with something on the brain other than what is edible, and if you don't find him, stay by yourself and get a few friends at the SPCA.

What did Mary Edna and I have in common all those years? We were the two girls at school who were not in what the teacher called "a traditional home." Every time that phrase was spoken people turned around in their seats and stared at us. Mary Edna grinned and waved at everybody like she might have been the homecoming queen, but I hated those moments. I kept saying to Mary Edna, "That kind of attention is *not* good," but she didn't hear a word I said. She believed then (as she still does) that any attention is better than nothing. And she got plenty of attention with botched-up marriages and unwanted pregnancies, one drug bust and one shoplifting scene (two padded bras and a lime green dickey from J.C. Penney). I told her I would have given her the money, maybe not for that ugly dickey, but for practical underwear items that she needed, yes, I'd've bought those. I told her that while she was out getting herself all the attention that she missed as a child because her parents were do-nothing alcoholics, her own children were suffering. But again, she did not seem to hear.

Mary Edna lived with her mother's various relatives and whoever from the church invited her home, and I lived with my grandma because my mother was too young to be a mother; my mother wanted a chance in life, and Grandma felt like she deserved that. I think of it as the chain reaction of mamas. Everybody is guilty; everybody is trying so hard to make up for her mama's failures. We all learn from one another. For example, my grandma used to always say "work like a nigger," and I had to preach long and hard for years to convince her that it did not sound nice. She said it wasn't racist because they *did* work hard, and I gave up explaining the point. Still, she has come around enough that now she'll get that *n* sound coming through her nose and then catch herself. Now she says things like "He works like a n-n-nun" or "She works like a noogie."

"A noogie?" I asked, and she waved her hand and said I knew what she meant. Grandma and I aren't where we should be but we keep on moving. She is all I have.

And come to think of it, I guess that's where my life differs from Mary Edna's. At her house everything was coarser, shakier. She claims her mother's first cousin never touched her but that she was always scared he might, that his face haunted her, and she discovered early that the more men she was with, the further she could get from that feeling. He is doing time by now, anyway. Her third ex-husband is probably the only person other than me and my grandma who ever really loved her, but he finally gave up and married a quiet, nearly homely woman from a neighboring town. I think he got as far from Mary Edna and her need to make somebody hurt her as he could—both of them running like rabbits, leaving the girls to stare out at the world with their round-eyed fear. They are four and five, dark-eyed beauties who deserve a hell of a lot better. I have thought of stealing them and driving to the west coast, except that would be one more example of running, and I think more than anything they need a spine of steel; they need to stand tall until they can safely walk forward. These days more kids are not in "a traditional home" than are—and those that are will one day go into a therapy office and say how very lucky they were, or they will say how the facade of a traditional family does not a traditional family make. There is no human with the answers.

Speaking of dysfunction and mama failures, I only met my mama once, and she was an absolute mess. My grandma said, "This is what I gave up my life for you to do?" My mama sat there like a big overstuffed chair, her toenails looking like she'd been digging potatoes. Mary Edna has always said that that's why she's big on painted toenails in the summer; you can hide the dirt. I told her that soap and water is another fine way to deal with the dirt—you can get rid of that dirt if you desire. That's what I wanted to tell my mama. I wanted to say, "Liberate yourself—shed that filth and pestilence." I wanted to tell her that mothers don't come with a warranty; that she could at least try to make it up to me. I was, after all, trying so hard to forgive her, especially if she bathed and did something with her hair. Her name is Ashley Amelia, and I had spent much of my childhood mooning over that name and creating wonderful romantic adventures for my mother in my head. The one picture my grandma had of her was from a high school yearbook where she looked no different from the other girls lined up there in the home ec class. My grandma could almost always kill a fantasy with warnings like "Things ain't always as they look, sound, or smell."

I recently read that all of these foreign people were given a list of English words and asked to select which one sounded most lovely. Nine out of ten people chose "diarrhea." This certainly seemed to fit my life. I hope those people weren't embarrassed when they found out what their chosen word meant. I hope they just shook their heads and laughed about how you just can't count on anything to be as it appears.

My mother was having trouble acting like a mother. It was more like she was my long-lost sister or cousin; she got along fine with Mary Edna. She showed us pictures of the latest man to dump her, and my grandma and I both shook in fear to see such an ugly face. For all the things my grandma had always said about the boy who had fathered me—a thick thatch of hair parted too far to the right, so that it pitched off like a rooftop (deceiving hair, because it made him seem sweet, when really he was the devil incarnate)—he was far superior to this thing in the photo. She stared down at his ugly face (even Mary Edna couldn't bear to look at the photo, said it stunk fumes off the paper) like she was in a stupor and said she didn't know why he treated her so bad. She said his words sometimes were so mean they cut her to the bone, though for the life of me I couldn't see a bone through that balloon of a body. I kept thinking that his words must have punctured, sliced like a knife does a melon. He ate what was edible and trashed the rest, and she had been rotting ever since, carrying that sweet, rotten smell of decay in her every pore and crevice. When she said she guessed she better head to the bus station, my grandma did not try to stop her, as I'm sure she wished somebody would. My grandma said she couldn't afford to keep her around and give her the liquor that without a doubt was close to killing her. Grandma said that when the time came, she wouldn't even need to be embalmed. I pictured this huge woman bottled up like those old pickled eggs they used to sell in the little grocery store down the road.

"My mama is all but dead," I kept thinking, and when she opened her arms to hug me, I felt like my heart was breaking. Here she was, already a ghost and replaced with this fleshy apparition.

If I was a child I might've been shuffled off to DSS but instead my friend Elizabeth, the third-grade teacher I am the assistant for, came and took me out to lunch, got me to talk about these things, cry a little bit. Elizabeth is a saint. If Mother Teresa had been five feet nine inches with wild red hair and was pro-choice, that would be Elizabeth. Sometimes I like to stand and look in through the glass of her front door and see her inside with her husband and baby; just this glimpse is all I need to make me hang on for what will be right for me. I want things to be clean, sober. I want Mary Edna to want the same things, but she is nowhere near seeing it all my way.

The only other thing I know about my daddy was told to me that day my mother came to visit. When he was a boy he had two cats he liked to torture. Their names were Uddnnnn and Errrrrnt, so that when my daddy went outside to call them, it sounded like a car wreck. A car wreck sounds like such a pleasant event compared to spending time with him. And why did somebody named Ashley Amelia choose such a loser? Maybe because her own mother threatened *her* husband that she'd kill him if he didn't take to the road and never return. There are some people who are not entirely convinced that my grandma *didn't* do something to him. Such is my legacy.

Way back, when I was on a scholarship at the junior college nearby and thought I needed to get married to be safe in this world, I often kept a boy in my room. I liked the way that a boy looked propped up on my bed, like something you might win at the fair. One of them was real cute but not too swift at all. A real limited vocabulary, limited mainly to *well I'll be goddamned* or *Ain't that some shit.* He was real handsome, when he was all cleaned up, but I couldn't stop thinking of his head as a maraca, like the ones I loved to shake in elementary school; he had little tiny specks of information rolling around in his head and making enough sound that he didn't seem like a zombie. Another boy who liked me a lot I let go, due to the fact he smelled like a chicken.

"Don't you know?" Mary Edna asked me while laughing hysterically. "All the unknown things in life taste and smell like chicken."

I said that I didn't say "chicken" but "*a chicken,*" like that coop we grew up down the road from. The smell of chickens in a coop has nothing in common with the Colonel and his seven secret spices. I told her that she had to change the way that she looked at men, that it was like upgrading your car or anything else in life. At the time she was dating a man whose idea of a good time was renting those red-shoe diary videos and ordering out for pizza. I met him once, and he invaded my space so entirely that I could smell his gingivitas. When I told Mary Edna this, she said I should be ashamed, like I might have really sniffed this jerk around the butt like a dog. I said, dental hygiene? You know bacteria, decay, death within life? Unflossed gums like an unplowed field. Rotten. She looked at me like I might be insane, and I thought then we had moved so far from each other that there was no hope of us ever conquering the world.

I love to floss my teeth. I like the thought of how you can take pulpy, unhealthy gums and floss them until they are tough and ready, no longer bleeding. There's enough blood in this world without what is unnecessary and completely avoidable. That's how I see the children I work with. Elizabeth has talked me into going back to school, and in a few years I'll have my own classroom. I might have Mary Edna's children with me.

I fall asleep at night while creating my future. I make my grandma color-blind. I tell her to give me a little bit of a smile, work those muscles so she will keep her face in shape, like old Jack Lelane—as ancient as he is, he keeps teaching. I give her a freezer full of frozen Baby Ruths (her very favorite), and I buy her that fancy sewing machine she has wanted forever. And then I start telling lies, as many of us do as a form of survival. I tell her that she ought to forgive herself for the way my mother turned out, that it wasn't her fault at all. I tell my mother that I'm sorry her life took such bad turns, that it wasn't her fault at all, that she could still climb up and out of that hole and start over. I tell her that just because your back tire gets stuck in a muddy field doesn't mean you ought to drive the whole car in. I give her a case of Ivory soap and thick nubbly washcloths to cleanse herself; I give her a new dress and a new hairdo and a daughter who in my opinion has turned out damn well. I tell her I wish I had the power to send her back to the time of that high school photograph and give her a second chance, but I can't. And that's what is really the sad part. I can't change a single thing in her past, and even if I could, I don't know now that I'd want to. Who knows where I would be if things had not happened as they did?

First, you recognize what was wrong, I tell Mary Edna's girls every chance I get, and then you *accept* it. This does not mean that you *agree* with it, just that you say, yes, that is what happened. And then you walk off and leave it there; it is not your mess to clean up. Right now I use that speech when I'm talking about the neighbor's dog who uses the sidewalk for his toilet, or when some child gets mad and throws toys around the room in a tantrum. But there will come a day when I have to say it in reference to their mother; I like to think they will be relieved.

A Blinking, Spinning, Breathtaking World

The temperature plummeted, and by late afternoon what had promised to be the beginning of the spring thaw refroze in slick, sloppy patterns, prompting radio deejays to warn drivers again and again that they should use caution, should prepare for long delays on the turnpike, should stay home if possible. The back roads were dangerous, especially in the suburban towns that refused to use salt. Charlotte lived in such a town. She rented a small, two-bedroom house at a very busy intersection. The house was so small it barely held her half of the marriage.

She played the radio at the end of every day while she cooked dinner—Stouffers for herself, Chef Boyardee for her six-year-old son. Station 93.7—hits of the seventies. It seemed the music was the background of her whole life. Sometimes it left her feeling hopeful, as if she was back in high school and worried only about a math quiz or a date for the football game. The radio was her spouse now, churning out words and rhythms to prompt her emotions. Meanwhile, Sam stared into the big colored screen, orange and blue with the Nickelodeon logo. The Eagles, America, Seals and Croft—*take it easy* and *summer breeze.* She often thought of clothes and record albums and turns of phrase her husband would not recognize as *her.* He didn't know *that* her; it was odd to think how often people must not *really* know their spouses. They know part of a person—the post–high school, postcollege, postdivorce person. Were the missing parts important?

It was in the afternoon that she most felt the cold; when the tendon in her upper thigh—thanks to an ancient hamstring pull—tightened like a knot. But there was more, an animosity, a fear. The cold set her teeth on edge as she looked out over that dark backyard just big enough for a swingset and sandbox. She was separated from her neighbors by a row of dark shrubs. The neighbors' sensor light switched on and off with the movement of the icy tree branches. The lights should have been a comfort, but instead they kept her alert, vigilant, waiting for something about to happen. Her paper was delivered and often remained untouched, the headlines too bleak for her to handle. People were snapping, committing the unthinkable. Crimes were described in too much detail. Like the au pair who shook a child to death. The man who was leading a double life—he murdered his girlfriend of five years and their child, then drove to the next town where his wife of three months was waiting for him. The young bride was so shocked by his arrest—*it's a mistake,* she screamed at reporters. Last night the word *murder,* smudged by damp plastic wrap, prompted her to toss the whole paper unopened into the garbage. The sensor lights went on and off and on and off, and she felt a chill as if someone or something out in the darkness of the yard were watching.

Last night had been warm. The sidewalks were slushy. Early crocus bulbs were trying to surface. It was supposed to stay warm, today and tomorrow; it was supposed to rain and wash away the last of the dirty gray ice outlining the yards. Oh, but *April fools,* the deejays began saying, promising snow, lots of snow, a nor'easter with inches and inches predicted for the next day. Phone lines and electricity could be downed. People should stay in, be careful, which translated to *get out to the store while you can.* Get your candles and sterno and firewood and flashlights. Charlotte had a closetful of supplies, which had prompted her husband to nickname her *the liberal survivalist.* He said that she was a woman prepared for all emergency situations. Bring on your storm, your power failure, your Nightmare on Elm Street. Now she went to the small stuffy basement to make sure her supplies were in place: water, batteries for the transistor, candles, flashlights, thermal blankets, astronaut food (Sam's contribution). She was prepared for everything except her current situation. How do you prepare for rejection?

They had planted crocus bulbs back in the fall, a last attempt at planning a future. He had never planted a bulb in his life and dug every hole meticulously, measuring with a ruler, sprinkling the bonemeal, topping with the mulch. She watched with fascination, hopeful of spring, an end to the bleakness, a welcoming to warmth. Now all over New England crocus tips were reaching up, trying to break out, and where were they? Not divorced and not together. Domestic purgatory.

She should have seen it as an omen that she'd met him at the Spooky Carwash on Route 9. The waiting line of cars wrapped out into the road, screeches and bad organ music mingling with the squeals of children and the sounds of swishing suds. Both of them were young and single. So why do young and single people go to the Spooky Carwash alone in late October?

"Car freak," he said. "And I like the entertainment."

"Feature article," she said, though at the time she had no idea that the local paper would actually run it. She wrote as a freelance while attending nursing school at night. They talked so long waiting in line that they agreed she would park her car and just ride through with him. It was a decision she was relieved to have made once they were inside the dark, scary tunnel. She grabbed his arm and held on until the idling car was pushed back out into the crowded lot.

Now the memory of the haunted house sounds and goblin faces gave her the creeps, and she went to close the drapes. There was a time when Jeff called to check on them. Are you in for the night? Are you okay? The calls both comforted and angered her. At first his voice pulled her back to the beginning and bathed her in a wash of promise, charming and witty and oh so concerned. She would feel herself near the point of begging; they could start all over. She would pretend that he had never cheated on her, something he still denied, as did all of their friends, who, she is certain, must have known *something*. Things don't just happen without any clues at all, do they?

Too late, he said, in so many words. *Too late.* And she knew in his dismissal that *his* life had never stopped moving. He got off one train and boarded another. He left his son behind like he might a piece of luggage. He'd come back with a claim slip one of these weekends.

"Can't we try?" she had whispered, Sam asleep in the next room. But his silence, his inability to look her in the eye was the answer. He could cry. He could express a sadness that the marriage had failed. What he couldn't seem to express is *why* it had happened—*how, when, and where* it had happened. How could he see it as a complete failure when she didn't? She felt stupid to be caught in such an ordinary situation.

"How did this happen?" her relatives kept asking, and when she responded "I don't know," they looked at her in a way that left her feeling guilty and responsible. She could hear the females clucking their tongues, determining that she must have fallen short on her wifely duties. Poor thing, Jeff, after all, worked so hard. Yes, all of those emergency dermatology calls. *If it's wet, dry it up. If it's dry, make it wet.* From the beginning, he went to this convention and that, and no one ever offered to come and help *her.* But just turn it around and look what happened—little helpers flew in like good fairies with casseroles and hours of free babysitting for him. There were no survival kits for what *that* made her feel like. So why is it that everyone seems to understand *why* he left her? Why don't they wonder why she didn't leave him?

She thought of those people who snap suddenly—or so it seems to the public—like the man who impaled his wife on a post in their well-landscaped backyard, all because his tostado was too hot. Or the one who forced his girlfriend to climb into a trunk in his attic and watch wild-eyed as he tore off lengths of silver electrician's tape to plug the airholes, to bind her wrists and ankles. All the papers. All the news programs. How many domestic cases? How many in the poor neighborhoods? Blue-collar? White-collar, like the hideous impaling, makes it to the front page.

Sometimes, at night, she sought comfort at the foot of Sam's bed; his little-boy breath, sighs in the night. She liked to walk Jingles, their old collie, early and then turn in for the night. But tonight she had promised him a night out, Papa Gino's, or one of those godawful indoor playgrounds. Phony worlds created to look wonderful from a distance. No sooner were they in the car with the heater going full blast, and battling bumper-to-bumper traffic as people made their way home for the blizzard weekend, than Sam began begging for Wonderland. The latest site of numerous birthday parties, it was a huge tin structure, converted from one of the wholesale clubs that had gone out of business, and there were enough fluorescent tubes inside and out to light an airport.

So much for people staying in for the night. The Wonderland parking lot was filled to capacity, and Charlotte had to drive to satellite parking across the street behind Computer City. She flipped on her car alarm and turned to pull Sam's hat into place and remind him that he was to hold her hand and walk quickly. She explained that it was icy and it was cold and they couldn't stay at Wonderland that long anyway.

They crossed the street and threaded their way through the icy lot, while she committed to memory where the car was parked—third row down, between a red pickup and a blue station wagon. She should write it down; she was forgetting so many details now. She was about to open her purse for pen and paper, but Sam was rushing her, wanting to get there. This was the kind of fun that Jeff (and whatever woman he asked to accompany him) gave Sam every other weekend. It was the kind of fun she would enjoy much more once it was over, when they were safely tucked back in—doors all locked, dog at the foot of the bed—and she could tell herself she'd given Sam a wonderful night out.

The outside of the building was painted with characters from Alice in Wonderland, advertising what was offered inside: the Mad Hatter's teaparty ride and the Queen's croquet court, the mirrored funhouse, and so on. The place had not been open long, and the building was still ringed by Porta-Johns and piles of rubbish. Sam couldn't wait to drop through the rabbit hole, a huge twisting slide through darkness. She thought she'd probably walk down. She was a technician who prepared people for their MRIs. She was the one who gave them Valium and talked soothingly. She had gone in once herself so that she'd know what she was talking about. It had felt like a coffin and she found herself consumed by irrational fears of no air and no light. Ever since, she had been careful to warn people seriously. She didn't just offer the drugs; she recommended them. *It will scare you to death,* she always wanted to say, *you will panic for air,* but she fought the urge. She couldn't afford to get transferred from her spot—there are very few nursing positions that don't involve much blood. She had passed out cold three times during nursing school; most recently it had happened when she clipped Jingles's toenail too close and sprayed blood all over the kitchen floor.

* * *

Sam was small for his age and his features looked fragile, more so because of the contrast of his thick, dark lashes against his pale face. He had her skin and Jeff's straight dark hair, Jeff's pale gray eyes. Whenever he pondered something—the reasons why they no longer live with his dad; Tiger, their cat, as she lay having kittens; or even this fun-filled park—his expression turned so serious that it made her want to cry.

Now she followed the concrete trail. Painted white-rabbit footprints led up to the door of the building. Despite her begging Sam not to run ahead of her, he was already up there, leaning against the turnstile where a family of five stood waiting to pay. The three children looked just like their mother, pale blond hair, plump white skin. Was the older, darker man the father?

Charlotte bought two passes, and they moved through the turnstile. Directly ahead was the rabbit hole. There was a ramp for those unable to slide, and she toyed with the idea of using it, but Sam was waiting for her. Would Jeff slide? Of course he would. She followed Sam into the long line, which was nearing the hole, slow step by slow step. Jeff would be coming to pick Sam up the next day. He was taking him for a week, spring vacation, another irony that the weathermen kept pointing out. It was the first time Sam would be away for more than two nights, and though she relished a little bit of quiet time, which she had not had in weeks, she couldn't imagine sleeping night after night in an empty house.

Before she could speak, Sam leaped through the hole and was gone, his happy scream spiraling after him in the tunnel. Charlotte felt the eyes of antsy children frustrated by slowness. "Come on," Sam was calling, and she surprised herself by stepping in, letting the tube take her body. The drop was much steeper than she'd anticipated. She heard herself screaming all the way to the bottom, a thick cushion of foam. She was out of breath, her neck tense. A man monitoring the landing yanked her forward just as another kid plowed down.

Sam was already in line for the Red Rose Ride, a piece of machinery with long spidery arms and carts that turned and spun at the end of each arm. It was the tallest ride in the building and they had raised the ceiling to accommodate it. When she was little she had loved this kind of ride, had thrilled to see rinky-dink carnivals stop in her hometown and within a few hours create a blinking, spinning, breathtaking world. On their honeymoon she and Jeff had ridden a roller-coaster that raced upside down through a dark tunnel; they had laughed at the sign warning those with heart problems to stay away. Now she caught herself studying the nuts and bolts that held one piece to another, the safety bar latches, and the rough-looking characters pulling the levers. Charlotte tilted her head and watched the arms weave and turn and the rosebuds spin. She heard the screams of the rosebud riders; she saw their arms waving and their hair flying. She looked up to see that the monstrous ceiling portrayed a summer sky, pale blue with puffy white clouds and streaks of sunshine.

"Are you sure you want to do this?" she asked Sam. He was nodding, his hand clutching the fabric of her shirt. He no longer grabbed *her,* just things attached to her, but her sister claimed this would have happened anyway, even if Jeff were home, even if there had never been the lengthy separation, the cold distant discussions. "He's just growing up," her sister said.

They slid into their designated rosebud and an attendant latched the safety bar. Charlotte could not keep herself from repeatedly checking it, lifting and pulling. She had to check and double-check, the same way she did the doors and windows of their house late at night. She watched the young boy who had locked them in. Was he really competent to pull that lever? Had there been any accidents here in Wonderland in its three months of existence? Had anyone's cart gone sailing through that fake sky?

With the blizzard coming, Charlotte thought Wonderland might be part of what Jeff had planned for the vacation week. For once she'd beaten him to the draw. She would have the pleasure of watching Sam have fun and she would leave the nausea and irritability following too much junk food and too little sleep for Jeff to deal with for once.

It will scare you to death, she wanted to tell him, but didn't he already know that? Wasn't fear why he had left to begin with—fear of getting older, fear of having a wife who was getting older, fear of staying aboard the same old train when others were hopping onto newer and faster engines? Charlotte closed her eyes and allowed her head to spin and spin with the words, with a vision of Jeff hearing all of this come from her, his look of surprise at her forcefulness. She brushed away her tangled hair, and saw Sam still clutching the safety bar. "Whew," she said and waited, not sure if he were about to laugh or cry. Joy or pain? High or low? She feared extremes and always had. If things were too good she waited for the bottom to drop out; if things were bad, she was overwhelmed by the energy required to climb back up. She thought living right in the middle was okay, but that was where they disagreed. *It's dead,* he said, meaning their marriage, even though she pretended not to hear and went to pull down and throw away a crusty brown philodendron on the bookcase. *Just accept it.*

Without thinking, she reached and pulled Sam up close to her, which jerked him to attention. He was aware of the older kids waiting in line as he pushed her away. "Wow!" he exclaimed. "Let's go again!"

They played a round of what was really miniature golf but was billed as croquet, and Sam won a free pass to play again. It seemed everyone won such a pass, or at least every kid did, so all that was needed was another ticket for the adult to play along. If only the children would suddenly unite and play together by themselves. Just behind them were a young boy with only one arm and a man whom she assumed was his father. The boy did amazingly well with just his right arm, and as he adjusted the club with his chin and then swung, Charlotte saw the stump of his other arm, which ended just below the elbow to leave him a slight el. A large dimple of skin had been pulled and tucked in like a navel. When Sam pushed her forward to the next hole—just beyond a line of aluminum cards bent in funny positions—she realized that the father had seen her staring. She looked away, ashamed, her face flushed. "Good one," the man yelled. The boy had not, in fact, gotten the ball in. He had merely touched it with the club, tapped it a few inches. She glanced at the man and found him gazing at her. His large brown eyes solemn, he gave her a slight nod, and then a smile, as if to reassure her that they were used to the stares, as if to tell her she hadn't done anything wrong. She nodded back and followed Sam to the eighteenth hole, where a large wooden cutout of the Cheshire Cat was set to flash lights and ring bells for holes-in-one.

Kindness was not something Charlotte had allowed herself to feel since the separation. She had severed all ties with their mutual friends, even those who wanted to remain close to her. She was afraid to trust anybody. If the person you sleep with every night can turn on you, why not an aquaintance? Why not a neighbor? When Barbara Reynolds called to check on her (she and Jeff had been in their wedding, and they'd been in their's), Charlotte had more or less told her that she didn't want to see them.

"But we're talking about years, Charlotte," Barbara said, her voice sounding high and unnatural, to Charlotte who cradled the receiver so that her hands could move freely through the medicine chest, discarding old razor blades and shaving cream. She poured out a bottle of aftershave Sam had given to Jeff for Father's Day; she knew even as she poured it out that she would spend the afternoon going back into the bathroom to catch what remained of the familiar scent.

"Well, I can't help that." Charlotte had said. She heard the shock and hurt in Barbara's voice, but it was as if she were reading a prewritten script. It was what she had to do to survive. Those who were really her friends would, she believed, welcome her back when it was all over and when she felt secure enough to return. It was a kind of test—*prove you are loyal.* "I'm starting all over and I mean from scratch."

Good, that's a boy." The man was patting his son on the back. His muscles rippled under the tight sleeves of his Grateful Dead T-shirt. The one-armed boy was begging to go on another ride, and the man stopped and turned to the side, pulled a thin canvas wallet from his back pocket and fingered the bills. She turned her head quickly, but again he caught her watching. His shoelaces were tied in big fat bows identical to the boy's and they wore their hair similarly, cut close and combed straight back.

She followed Sam to the snack bar, where they ordered hot dogs and drinks. They sat at a picnic table under enormous signs that said "Eat Me" and "Drink Me." Nearby was a petting zoo, a series of too-small open-lidded cages: a pathetic flamingo, two white rabbits, some mice, a couple of goats, and a frightened baby tiger. While Sam ran from cage to cage, she sat on a bench and studied the crowd: the excited children and their parents worn out from another work week and dreading the snow-shoveling they'd have to do the next day. The pale, plump family was squeezed around one table sharing two huge pizzas. Charlotte watched as all five roared in laughter at something the youngest had said. The youngest looked exactly like the father when he laughed. When the manager of Wonderland (a large man with a bad toupee) stopped by to see if the family needed anything, the father responded quickly with a wave of his hand that they didn't need anything else. "We're just fine," he said, and Charlotte felt a great twist of envy over the pronoun *we,* over his speaking on behalf of the others—on behalf of his family.

She caught herself hoping for a blizzard that would keep Jeff's girlfriends away and leave him stranded all alone with Sam. She thought of Sam tossing and twisting throughout the night, missing his own bed. Of his middle-of-the-night cries of "But I *can't* sleep!" But when Sam came running up to get her attention, to make sure she watched while he actually *touched* the tiger, she asked herself what she was doing, wishing misery on him, when all she really wanted was for Jeff to say that he was sorry, it was a mistake; he had taken her for granted, would she *please* take him back.

She turned to see a man in a Wonderland suit (she guessed they were all meant to look like the Mad Hatter) standing by Sam as he stroked the poor little tiger. She felt a rush of fear and then there was the man with the one-armed boy, waiting their turn. Again the father nodded to her as if to assuage her fears before letting his own son offer up his one good arm to the creature.

The boy also had a scar along his neck, visible now that his sweat-slicked hair was pushed back and off to one side. She had tried to imagine the birth of the child, the pronouncement of his deformity to the parents. She had wondered if such a thing made a marriage stronger, pulled two people closer, begged that they hold each other in the night when they woke to discover that what they hoped was a nightmare was real. But maybe it wasn't a birth defect. Now, it looked more like the result of an accident. A car crash? Icy roads? Was the mother lost on some back road along with the boy's arm? Or had he gotten too close to some horrible machine? She realized that she had been holding her breath, that she had failed even to notice the pale family of five go back to order two more pizzas.

"Did you *see* me?" Sam asked as he raced up, his shoe untied and dragging the ground. "Wait till I tell Dad."

Their last ride of the night was through the house of mirrors. They squeezed into a tiny cart on a track. The cart was deep, the sides so high passengers could see only what was directly in front. What Charlotte could see was that the man and the one-armed boy were in the next cart up. She heard them talking; the boy said he was tired, that he wanted to go home. Then there was a whir of machinery and their carts split and turned, racing toward this mirror and then that. Everywhere she looked she saw her face beside Sam's, long and thin, round and fat, their eyes huge, like insect eyes. She strained to watch other people pass, normal faces, and managed to catch sight of a teenage couple she had seen kissing at one of the tables earlier; she glimpsed little children, sunk down in the huge seats, the safety bars seeming apt to decapitate them as they twisted and turned, eyes held wide in alarm and fear. Sam grabbed her now. He reached his hand over and held tightly to her arm, and she grabbed him back closing her eyes to the dizzying mirrored spin. He gripped her the same way that she had always gripped Jeff. Every year they had returned to the Spooky Car Wash to celebrate the night they met, and every year she would shriek and lean away from the windows where ghoulish faces appeared along with suds and brushes. The year Sam was three they had to honk the horn and beg the goblins to back off; he was wailing in the back seat and even when they drove to Friendly's for ice cream and sat with him huddled up in the front seat between them eating his ice-cream cone, he continued to sniff and cry and refused to look at them. The next year they got a babysitter and left Sam at home, and the year after that he loved it so much they went through twice. She should have known when Jeff was too busy to go last year that everything was not as good as it seemed.

She was dizzy by the time the carts began to slow and filed back onto the track. It was still dark, but she heard the one-armed boy again. *Let me go,* he said, and then the machinery screeched and whined. *Please, Mister.* Mister? Wasn't he the father? Wasn't he the person in charge? She thought she heard *Shut up;* she thought she heard *I'll break your goddamn neck,* but the PA system was announcing the license number of a car with its lights on and that it was one hour until closing. And there was old disco music blasting from the video arcade. She blinked against the bright fluorescent lights, the swarms of people in line for this ride, that game. A group of older children was dancing to that song, "YMCA." She looked at Sam to see if he had heard what she heard, but he was laughing and begging to go again; everyone was laughing, talking, sighing with relief. She glanced up just in time to see the man and the boy exit the ride and head through the crowd. They walked fast, the man pulling the boy along. What had she witnessed? A threat? A warning? Her mind raced, conjuring every horror show she'd ever seen, every hideous news story. These evil people appeared normal on the surface, but then enough time passed for neighbors' voices, and relatives', to worm out of the woodwork, to remember that the person was antisocial, had a volatile temper, had tortured animals as a kid, had no conscience, no respect for others. Were people guilty when they turned their heads and ignored all the signs? Was she?

They stumbled out of their cart and down the ramp, but by then the man and the boy had disappeared in the crowd. Though Sam begged for another ride, she dragged him by the hand up to the food counter and quietly tried to explain to the woman serving the sodas that she had heard a man threatening a child. "I threaten mine all day long," the woman said and sighed. "If you don't do this, I'll never let you out of this house again." Her lips turned downward as she reached to fill another cup.

The young security guard at the exit smiled at Charlotte while she stood near him, trying to decide if she should say anything to *him*. And what *was* he supposed to do? What was *she* supposed to do? Why would the guard be any more trustworthy than anybody else in the world? She shivered. In her mind, many minutes had already passed—enough time to pull a boy into a car, to tie him up, to slit his throat, to toss him out like a sack of garbage on the turnpike.

In spite of his protests, she pulled and held Sam close

as they lingered in the false comfort of the building. The huge fans were pumping in so much heat that children were sweaty and trying to get out of the coats their parents had just wrestled them into. She got her keys from her purse, set her finger on her alarm whistle, and convinced herself that it was not such a far walk. They would do it quickly, briskly. She would tell Sam they had to walk fast because it was so cold out and the blizzard was coming. In fact the snow was already starting, earlier than expected. Fine flakes and drops of frozen rain were falling on the cars' roofs and hoods. Already there was the silencing effect of the snow, and by tomorrow there would be three feet or more, drifts up to doors and windows. Jeff's new sports vehicle would allow him to pick Sam up right on time. She would be stranded.

She set their quick pace through the parked cars, eyes straight ahead, though she was aware of every sound. She kept expecting to see the man and the boy; she was expecting the worse. They crossed the slippery street and entered the empty satellite lot. She imagined figures crouched behind fenders, hiding under the driver's side and then reaching out and grabbing her by the ankle. Where was the car? What row? What row? She panicked. She pressed the button on her alarm, intentionally setting off her own car so that it wailed and called to her from the darkness. "Hurry, hurry," she said, and they ran toward the car down at the far end of the lot, windows already covered in a fine layer of white. She didn't turn her face to Sam's, afraid that he would see her fear and stop running. She wrenched open the car door on her side and pushed him in—too *hard,* he complained—and she slammed her door and pressed the automatic lock. The engine turned easily, and then she was able to let go and cry. She had reached the bottom of the long dark hole and now she would either remain there or begin working her way back to the surface. There was no magic potion; no incantation to make the world stop blinking, stop spinning. She could only hope that her body would keep moving—slow step by slow step—to the lines for the rest of the breathtaking rides. But for now, she was scared frozen, scared to death.

PART III

Your Husband Is Cheating on Us

Your husband is cheating on us. I'm assuming that he hasn't told you yet. I'm the test wife and he tries everything out on me first, I mean *everything.* Remember when he got hooked on that massage oil that heats up with body temp? Now maybe you liked it, but I sure didn't. I got a rash, but of course, I have extremely sensitive skin and always have. I mean, I am Clinique all the way. If you were writing up this triangle (fast becoming a rectangle), then *you'd* be the one with sensitive skin, the fair, hothouse flower, and I'd be the scrub grass by the side of the road.

And look at you—some tan. I know that you go to Total Skin Care and get in the sunning beds. It's odd how he tells me all about you. There have been many times when I've said, well, why don't you just go on home then? And of course, that's the ironic part, because he always does. But, girl, like are you thick? I would *know* if my man had been out messing around. Like I know your perfume—Chloe—and the fact that you have not picked up on my Shalimar is amazing. I wear the stuff the way it's supposed to be worn—heavy; I'm one of those women people ask not to be seated next to on the airplane. At my last clerical job they ran a ban on perfume in the workplace after I'd been there a week, so I had to quit on principle. That's me, a quitter; a principled quitter. When the going gets tough I get the hell out, always have.

I've come here today with a proposition for you, but before I get into that, I thought you might like to hear a bit about me. I'd think you'd want to, given that I know everything there is to know about you. I know your mama died last January, and I have to tell you that I almost called you up to give my condolences. I mean, I'd been hearing about how awful her illness was and how you were traveling back and forth to tend to her. I heard you on the answering machine many times when I'd be over here cooking dinner. I've got to tell you that I just love your kitchen—that commercial-size stove and those marble countertops. Was he feeling guilty when you all remodeled, or what? You and I both have excellent and very similar tastes. Don't look at my hair. It's not a good day. You should see me when it's just cut and blown dry. Maybe I can show you some time.

Anyway, one of those nights when I heard you on the machine, you were crying so hard that I almost picked up, so strong was my urge to want to comfort you. When Mr. Big got home, I told him there was a message I felt he had to listen to right that minute, and of course, he did, but then did he call you? No, ma'am. And did he call to check on your son, who he had dumped off at the Anderson house and them not even home from work yet? I told him that if I had a son I believe I'd be more responsible with him, and he just pawed the air like I might be dumb. He must do that to you a lot, too. I'm sure he must. I even suggested I excuse myself, go to the mall or something so he could have his privacy but he just waved again and shrugged, like, ayyhh. Well, that was the first time I stopped and asked myself just who in the hell was this man I was sharing my (or *your*) bed with? I looked at him in a completely different way after that. I mean, how could he hear you sobbing and carrying on like that and not rush to call you? I see your surprise and I'm sorry. We all grow up and find out that the truth hurts. But here's some truth you might like. I did *not* sleep with him in your bed that night. I faked myself a migraine (complete with blinding aura) and made him drive me straight home. Do you think *he* ever looked all around to make sure your neighbors weren't looking? Hell, no. Either too stupid or just didn't give a damn, I can't figure which. I moaned and groaned and talked of the bright lights I was seeing out of my right eye (I told him the left had already shut out in complete blindness), and honey, he drove faster than the speed of light. I have always noticed how men (at least the ones I've come into contact with) can't stand to observe pain. It just sends them right up a tree. I have also faked menstrual cramps with Mr. Big on several occasions, and so I know in great detail (he talks a hell of a lot, doesn't he?) that you have just terrible periods and always have. My bet is that you've faked your share, am I right? Well, either way, I know how you sometimes ask him to crush up some Valium into some juice that you sip through a straw so you don't have to sit up and straighten yourself out. Genius. Make that Mr. Big Ass work! But honey, I'm not so sure I'd trust him, you know? If I were you I might mix my own cocktails.

But enough about that, I wanted to tell you about me. Get yourself a drink if you like, or a cigarette. I know you smoke. He knows you smoke, even though you think he doesn't. I mean, the man is slow for sure, but he isn't completely out of the loop. He has smelled it in your hair, even though he says you spray lots of hairspray and perfume (*he* doesn't know you wear Chloe—I do). So come on out in the open and just smoke. I smoked for years and I absolutely loved it. But I quit years ago. I am actually one of those who quit because of Yul Brynner coming on television and saying that, when I saw him there doing that ad, then it meant he was dead. Lord. That was a moving experience. I was holding a cigarette in my hand and was seven months pregnant (yes I have had a life, too), and I felt like Yul was looking directly into my eyes. Talk about an aura. Yul had an aura, and don't be like Mr. Big and make a joke about his baldness. I felt his soul reach out and grab me by the throat and say, *Put out the butt.* I went out on my back stoop, took one final drag (a long, delicious drag), and then I thumped that butt clean across the darkened backyard where it twinkled and glowed for just a brief second before dying.

If I was somebody who could like have one cookie at a time or could eat the designated portion written at the top of the recipe or on the side of the box, then I'd ask you to give me a cigarette, but we know better. If I had one cigarette, I'd have a carton. I have always told people that if I was ever given the bad news that my number had been drawn in that great bingo game we call fate and I only had a little bit of time left, that I'd get me a cooler of beer and a carton of cigarettes and several bottles of Hawaiian Tropic (the oil with the red label for tropical-looking people), a tape deck with all my favorites from when I was a teenager: Pet Clark and Chad and Jeremy, you know my time, I'm a few years older than you, I think. And I'd just stretch out and offer myself to the sun; a burnt offering. Burnt, greased, and buzzing like a bee.

The baby? You're asking about *my* baby? Well, let's just say that if I had a baby then my last wish would be a very different one. But that's not something I like to talk about. I'll tell you what I did come to talk about. You see, I have been thinking that we should get rid of Mr. Big. That's right, don't look so shocked until you hear me out. It would be just like in that movie that came out a year or two ago, only I do not want to get into a lesbian entanglement with you. I mean, no offense or anything, it's just not my cup of tea. Actually I would like some of whatever you're drinking. Diet Coke is fine. Don't slip me a Mickey, okay? A joke, honey. That's a joke. I'm full of them. Probably every joke you've heard over the past eight years has been right from my mouth. Mr. Big has no sense of rhythm or timing—in *anything,* you know?

Truth is you look a far sight better than how he painted you, and you look a damn lot better than that photo of you all in that church family book. I mean it made me sick to see Mr. Big Ass sitting there grinning like he was the best husband in the world when of course I knew the truth. Honey, there are facts and then there are facts, and the fact is that he is a loser with a capital *L.*

Arsenic is big where I'm from. I guess anywhere you've got a lot of pests there's a need for poison, and then maybe your perception of what constitutes a pest grows and changes over the years. There was a woman from a couple of towns over who went on a tear and fed arsenic to practically everybody she knew. If she had had herself a religious mission like Bo and Peep or Do and Mi, whatever those fools were called who tried to hitch a ride on the comet by committing suicide in new Nikes, or like that Waco freak, or, you know, that Jim guy with the Kool-Aid down in Guyana, she'd have gotten a lot of coverage—*People* magazine, *Prime Time,* you name it. When they finally wised up to her, she had enough ant killer stashed in her pantry to wipe out this whole county. It's big in this state. Cyanide, too, might be good because you've got that whiff of almond you might could hide in some baked goods. But I don't know how to get that.

I know what you're thinking, sister. I've been there. You see, your husband has been faithful to me for eight long years, and why he up and pulled this stunt I don't know. Middle-age crazy, I suspect. Maybe he wanted somebody younger and shapelier. Maybe he wanted somebody a little more hot to trot like my oldest friend—practically a relative—who sleeps with anybody who can fog a mirror, and her own little lambs fast asleep in the very next room.

If I had had my own little lamb, my life would have been very different. And I was going to tell you about the real me, so I'll just begin before I go back to my plan. You keep thinking about it while I do my autobiography for you. You see, I think that my first knowledge that I would live the life I do is when I was in the eighth grade and my foot jumped right into a size nine shoe. Now I'm looking over and I see that you are about a seven and a half, which is a very safe place for a foot to be these days. That's a safe size. But I hit nine so fast and all of the women in my family said, "Where did she get that foot?" My brother called me Big Foot. My great-aunt said, "Oh my God in heaven, what if she grows into those?" This from a woman who was so wide, her butt took up a whole shopping aisle at the CVS. I mean, it isn't exactly like I came from aristocracy but they thought so, or at least they thought that a slim little petite foot meant that somebody way, way back stepped off the boat in some size fours.

I maxed out at a size ten when I was a senior in high

school. There they are, full-grown pups, and honey, there isn't a single shoe on the market that I don't order and wear. Sometimes I have to order a ten and a half (I firmly believe that this is the result of the Asian influence in this country). I finally got to an age where I could look out at the world and say, "Fine—I am of good solid peasant stock; I am earth woman, working the fields, turning the soil." I can dig with my hands, and I can dig with my feet. My folks aren't sitting out on the veranda as much as they'd like to be. They are picking cotton and tobacco leaves, and when they get their tired hot bodies back to the shanties at the edge of the field, then here comes The Mister from the Big House. I know that might sound stupid to you, but the size of my feet made me both tough and subservient. I thought long ago that it could all turn around with me meeting the right person at the right time, but that has yet to happen.

You know when I first met Mr. Big, though, I thought it might be happening. Part of the reason I liked him so much that first time is because he talked a lot about you and your son, and he really did seem to care. I even asked him the first time we met in a more personal way, you know, didn't it bother him that he was cheating on you. He said at the time that it was okay because you were cheating on him; I let it be an excuse because he did look pretty cute back then, but I think I knew that you weren't really having an affair. I mean, you had a one-year-old. Now, I've never had a one-year-old but I sure do read enough, and know enough folks who do, that I know the odds of you having time to run around were out of the question. You were probably lucky to get a shower, am I right?

He showed me a picture of your son the first night I ever met him—a cute little thing, plump and grinning—but after we started sleeping together he never showed me any more pictures of your boy. Or you for that matter, other than Mr. Big's Holier Than Thou Church Photo. I should have known to leave him alone right then. I should have said *kiss off* and disappeared. And I'm still not entirely sure why I stayed, except that I was very lonely and I knew that he was safe.

I'm still lonely. I know you might think I'm putting too much stock on the size of my feet, but in my mind it is a physical symbol of my difference in my family. They are all over there in the nice warm room lit by firelight, and I'm way off yonder by the barbed-wire fence with snow on my boots while I shiver and peep in. I've always felt that way, and therefore I'm comfortable with it. I used to get hopeful every now and then, but I got over it.

And this woman! She is much younger than you are, honey. And she has got boobs such that you could place a cafeteria tray there (man-made, I'm sure). Short skirts. Over the knee boots, I mean, really. Everybody says I have awful taste in clothes, and I do much better than she does. I mean to tell you Mr. Big has hit bottom. Here he had us, two perfectly good-hearted, good-looking women, and he falls for *that*? If I were you, I might even take precautions against disease. She might be packaged to look clean, but that is one sordid thing. Check her out some time. I have her working schedule at Blockbuster's, and I know her address and phone number. As a matter of fact I've already started in harassing her for you. Don't thank me. I'm doing it for me, too.

So, I say we bump him off. Real easy. Slip him the poison. Start in small doses and then up it and up it until he's so sick with what seems to be the flu or some awful stomach problem and then we either choke or smother him, say he did it while trying to be a pig and eat while you weren't around. If you carry it through, you know, fall completely apart—grieve, rage, mention that hussy whore girlfriend down at Blockbuster, don't tamper with the will (a document that does not make a single mention of me!), then they'll believe you. Then just say that you feel you've got to get that man in the ground as quickly as possible.

Done. Then you go on about your business and I go on about mine and they might put Miss Blockbuster in the slammer. Truth is that I don't have much business and never have.

I almost had a baby one time. The daddy was nowhere to be found. Get up and shake the sheets, and he'd blown clean out the window and down the road, never to be heard from again. Well, here came a baby. Everybody kept telling me to get rid of it, but when have I *ever* done what anybody said to me? Never. So I plodded along, planning. I had lots and lots of plans. But it was a bad joke—a fake baby. No breath, no heartbeat. I looked at it and realized that was my life. No breath, no heartbeat. No life for me. I'm a slave girl—a servant. I'm one rung lower than a dog.

Mr. Big is too low to be called a dog; that would be an insult to canines everywhere. He didn't call you back that time. He was never there for me, not that I ever expected it; but what if just once he had been? What if just once somebody had taken better care of me, taken me to a real doctor, gotten some help. And Mr. Big knows that you've been feeling down lately, but does Mr. Big care? No. I say we kill him.

Oh, but I see doubt in your eyes. I see love, and for

that I sure am sorry for you. You better lose that light, honey.

Bring him down. Think of Delilah. Cut off his strength and watch him go blind and pull a building down on himself. Sap him while you can.

Oh, my, stop crying. Lord. I didn't come over here for this. You are not the woman I thought you were from that photo in the church book. You looked to me in that picture like a woman who could enlist in a complicated plot, but you are a bundle of jumpy weepy nerves. I know that we'd no sooner put Mr. Big down under, but what you'd be confessing and giving out my name. You are a tattletale. You were probably one in school and you're still one. I still call and hang up on the tattletale from my school, that's how much I hate a tattletale.

Oh, yeah, I can see it all, now. You're sitting there thinking about how you could nail *me*. The wife would get it easy. A woman under stress conned by the mistress. You're crazy if you think I'd fall for that one. I may not have any children to worry over, but I have pride. I have dignity. I have the child I almost had and lots of times that keeps me in line. I imagine where he'd be right now, twelve years old—my son waiting for me to get home so he can complain about what I don't have in the refrigerator. I tell people, maybe men I might've just met, "Oh no,

I don't stay out late. My son will be waiting for me." Don't think I don't know what it feels like. I was pregnant. I had mood swings. I studied all those wonderful little pictures of the fishy-looking baby growing legs like a tadpole—moving from water to land, just that easily.

But you have everything for real. You have Mr. Big legally.

You are hopeless, woman. I'm the one that ought to be crying! Snap to. Listen to some good advice, because in a minute I'll be out of here. You tell him that you know all about that little bitch he's been seeing (she works at Blockbuster Video and wears way too much eye makeup). Tell him he better shape his butt up or you are out of here, sister. Make him sweat. I mean I don't want a thing to do with him, you know? So use me. Call me by name. Tell him I'll come to your divorce hearing and help you clean up. Get him back if you want him, and make him behave. But don't let him off easy. Pitch a blue blazing fit. Scream, curse, throw things. Let him have it, honey. Your husband is cheating on us. Let him have it. And when all is said and done, please just forget that I was ever here; that I ever walked the earth. After all, I'm Big Foot. Who knows if I even exist.

It's a Funeral! RSVP

I have spent my life looking for the right occupation and have finally found it: I throw funerals. My husband, James, now has a good answer for all those people who ask what his wife does. *Well, she used to throw pots, and now she throws funerals.* That's true. Every phase of our marriage is neatly catalogued by my quest. Early on, I hand painted china figurines to mark life's special occasions (those were the pregnant years, and it felt good to sit on a pillow with my legs splayed and a fan blowing full in my face while I moved a teeny-tiny ox-bristle brush). When my children (a set of twin boys with a baby sister right on their heels) threatened my whole career every time they ran through the dining room, where I kept the several hundred figurines, they prompted me to design and build sandboxes and little frog ponds. That led me to a full-blown landscaping business, which, from time to time, included a sideline—a tree house–building service. All of that ended one hot summer of black thumbnails and complaining children (they had the Swiss Family Robinson tree house in mind and found my prefab four-by-six with loft to be seriously lacking). I realized I liked tending my own garden but had no real interest in anybody else's. Then I started catering, given that I was always in the kitchen anyway.

"So what now?" James asked at dinner the night of the baby's first day of kindergarten. I was left at home all by myself for the first time in eons. It was so quiet the first year I got two little Yorkies to keep me company. They yapped in stereo all day long; sometimes their yapping took the shape and rhythm of old hymns and I'd swing around believing they had just done two stanzas of "Softly and Tenderly." Now, when I look back, I think I was getting a signal, a sign. I did *not* tell James this, of course; he is a brain surgeon (yes, and don't laugh even if it is funny, and don't ask if I was a patient, as many do); we do not see eye to eye on the theory of thought process.

For me, the brain is a great big filing cabinet with memories packed into every crease and crevice. And every single memory is a key that unlocks the heart, a door that swings forward and lets in a rush of passion. *Without the heart that brain is worth nothing,* I like to say, and James nods, though I know from the look in his eyes that he is somewhere else, not really at our Queen Anne mahogany dining table that my son painted a yellow line (in oil paint) down the middle of to play race car the first day I got it. What is true, of course, is that James's profession has always paid for mine, until, of course, this last one, which is bigger than anybody ever dreamed it would be. I call it my "career of a life *and* a death time."

I speak of salvation and James speaks of sutures. He says a lot of men have asked him over the years how he can be married to a woman who runs around doing whatever she damn well pleases at all hours of the day. I knew *which* man said this. The same one who keeps his wife in little outfits from Neiman Marcus so she thinks she's getting a good deal while he bosses her butt around all day long. He once asked me at a dinner party what made me think I could do everything. This was right after he had just worn my ear to a nub talking about the tree house he built his sons, the oil painting he sold while still a mere college student, the poetry that he's sure would be printed in the *New Yorker* if he could just find time to send it out. It was clear as a bell to me that I was engaged in an arm-wrestling event I had not signed up for. I answered that I was proud for him. And I mentioned that I give myself a pap smear every now and again, and that I am frequently called in to estimate dilation of the cervix. He made a face at me, and I was then struck by all the garbage in this life. Here was a man not even forty who assumed he could do whatever anybody else was doing, but God forbid they attempt to do *his* business.

"I guess she'll be operating soon," he said to James in passing, and James in his normal completely checked-out way said, "Probably so." I found a way to get back over near where he was before leaving to say that I had also performed numerous rectal exams, that I had just that minute done one and found him to be the biggest one I'd ever encountered.

I know I'm rambling, but it's important that I lead you to the moment of realization and the reason I do what I do. Like a personal testimony, you know? I was about to turn forty and already many of my very favorite people were dead. I had children, and I wanted them to grow up with a clear vision of hope. A sense of nature and art and all that has walked this earth before them. But what I was getting was life in the nineties—can you do this? can you do that? can you do this? can you do that? Help me! Help me! comes the plea, but when you get there, the person who needed you so desperately can't decide what shoes go with the purse, can't decide how much lamb to buy. I was sliding to that point where my bones were feeling picked, every bit of flesh stripped away, just as I imagined was happening to my dear ones tucked in beneath the earth. There are people out there who will use you, eat you alive if you let them. They might as well say, "Hey, I'm going to a party, want to get wasted, want to borrow your brains, heart, liver, and lungs just for the occasion!"

I was feeling close to a breakdown. If I'd had time, I might have had one. I've seen that done. I had a great-aunt who had three hysterectomies over the course of her later life. The Everready Hysterectomy. It's like the college student with the grandfather who just keeps dying and dying and dying. I told James I might want to have a hysterical pregnancy followed by a complete fake hysterectomy, or, I told him, I could go someplace like Canyon Ranch Spa and take a nice long mud bath. I think I could manage that. I see myself propped up in a satin bedjacket (mineral water/carrot sticks/velvet drapes/classical music at tubside), or hell, let's get real. Send me to the Holiday Inn; Lanz flannel shrunk up to my shins, Diet Coke and sea-salt-and-vinegar chips. I'd eat until my mouth was parched and dry and then chase them down with cola. I'm a Taurus, and we do things like that—

chug, eat huge desserts, hug and kiss perfect strangers who look like they need some attention, seize ourselves by the horns.

I know people who sigh in tiredness at the end of a day of doing nothing. She might have one child that comes with a built-in babysitter, and she sighs, "Oh dear, I'm afraid I really have to leave the house for the cleaning service." Excuse me, like did I miss some big chunk of evolution? At the same party where Mr. OB talked so much I overheard someone ask, "Who's your girl?" I thought for a nanosecond that I was eavesdropping on a lesbian revolution out in suburbia, but no, it was the female version of who has the biggest penis. For women, it's who is the busiest in this culture-filled world. Does your child speak one language or three? When did he give up reading *Time* for the *New Republic?* An op-ed in crayon? Really? Do you do suzuki? Do you do soccer? Do you do liquor at the end of the day? (That was my line.)

I was there. I heard that. Whatever happened to children stretched out in the sunshine with their bookbags tossed off to the side. I loved that kind of day—the sun so hot it made a red, wriggly movie right there on your own eyelids; it made those file drawers fly open, the crevices in my brain responding to that slow Southern sun and melting with memory. Sometimes it felt so good, it made me have to pee, and sometimes if I was completely overwhelmed, I'd slip into the edge of the woods and pull down my underwear and lean there against a pine tree, my saddle shoes pretending to be the banks of the river—*Yellow River* by I. P. Freely, *Miniskirts* by Seymore Hiney. When you let your brain run, there are wonderful things to find. That's what I tell my children. Our old labrador, Trixie, a creature I brought into our marriage—one of the few creatures who cannot under any circumstances be taught to be aggressive—piddle-peed her whole puppyhood. She couldn't help it; it felt so good when she was happy. Even now when I take her out, right at six thirty, and she splays those lovely legs to pee, there is a look of complete relief and pleasure in her eyes. She knows what to be thankful for, and it is simple.

Children and dogs—we could all take a lesson. And that's what I was thinking, on those days right before my business started. Look, listen. See what the world can teach you. I filled myself up on the writing of Mr. Carl ("Young") Jung, which my whole life I had heard in my head as *Joung*. I even once made up a skipping-rope rhyme for my daughter where I said, "Carl *Joung* eats junket on the jungle gym." I figure he would forgive me this error. I got all into thinking of patterns and synchronicity and how at some great supreme level it all will come together. Just follow the life and learn all that you can.

I kept thinking of my good friend Marjorie, an older woman who lived across the street. The children called her "the cake lady," because she appeared at every school or church function bearing a gift of a cake in some shape or another. I knew she was failing when she appeared at the synagogue with a cake in the shape of a cross, purple icing draping the sides and a spray of frosted lilies in the center. I was there that day, as I have made it my business to visit a lot of different places. I asked, "But what difference does it make?" when I saw Marjorie there by the door with a look of complete bewilderment on her face. Apparently it *did* make a difference to some, not all, but enough that I drove Marjorie over to the Episcopal church, where it seemed she had earlier delivered a lovely Star of David, with strict instructions that the little silver balls were just for decor and not edible. That cake was still wrapped up and off in the tiny pine-scented kitchen. They loved the cross; they ate it up, and we ate the Star of David ourselves back at our house with Marjorie and her husband.

There are times when I have a wave of knowing, of seeing what is happening, and this was one of those times. Marjorie was sweaty with embarrassment but laughing about her mishap and James's joke about "you are what you eat." He asked what she would do for the Buddhists. The Muslims. She said then that she needed to bake herself a cake, but did not know how to shape senility. How do you shape forgetting? "You're the brain man," she said, and I knew from the way James was looking at her and the subtle questions he asked, parceling them carefully, no more than one question per course, that there would be some very bad news. As we sat with coffee and the Star of David cake, I heard him suggest that she have a few tests *just to rule out anything.* Her husband went pale with knowledge, and Trixie sat by her side as if frozen. Even the Yorkies knew not to yap, though they certainly knew that in minutes all three would get to lick up the last of the star.

Babies and dogs see things we don't. They respond to spirits and waves of emotion that we don't sense. James, of course, says it's just that their thoughts are not complex and therefore they appear to be fixated and entertained by things that aren't there. This is where our paths diverge, where he tends to the mechanics, greases those file cabinet drawers, removes the little tiny piece that got itself wedged in and prevented the drawers from opening. That's what he did to Marjorie, and then I stepped in to watch and help her pull all that she could from her files. I wanted to help her make sense of her life and if possible sense of the world. And Marjorie did make sense. The last conscious day of her life, I went over with some lunch, and she was there, sitting up in bed in a fine, yellow silk bedjacket that she'd bought for herself at Dillard's in Raleigh before going over to Durham for her first chemo. She told me she was writing out her service and would like very much for me to listen to it all and critique what she had done. She wanted the Beatitudes—blessed are those who mourn, those who hunger and thirst for righteousness. . . . And she wanted Psalm 30 about the joy that cometh in the morning. She wanted "We Gather Together" sung, because she loved Thanksgiving and all that it represented, even though she was grossly disappointed the one time she made it all the way up north to see Plymouth Rock, only to find it cracked and covered in graffiti. She believed in keeping the past pure, and she loved the last line: *He forgets not his own.* She said she'd come to believe that remembering was the greatest joy in life and without that power fully intact, it was easier to leave. "My plug has been pulled," she said and laughed. And then she told me how she had known it was bad even before she was told. She had felt it deep inside.

"I just got up one morning, went to the market and started cooking turkeys and hams—I baked pecan pies and pineapple upside-down cakes. Holidays." She sighed and leaned back on her pillow, turned away from me to her wedding picture on the wall, two young figures in black and white. Talking food was what we often did but I realized this was not about the food at all. "I've got his holidays done for the next several years. I labeled them, made enough for him to have our children and their children join him." She turned back to me then, her lip quivering as her hands fluttered in the air as if she were chasing little dust motes. "In every little container of giblet gravy, there is frozen a vial. I got these vials every time I ever bought saffron—like gold that spice, and I love it, tiny threads the color of the sun and the smell! Heaven. I saved the little bottles, and now there are messages there. I tell a joke. I give them my love. I tell them to hug and kiss one another and pretend that it is me." When I left she was sleeping there beside her weeping husband, his hands clutching hers to keep her from flying away.

The truth is that I have never admired anything quite so much in my entire life. At the time, my catering had taken a little slump. Instead of getting the good gigs like so-and-so's coming out as a debutante at the country club or so-and-so's getting married, I was basically doing meals-on-wheels for the elderly and shut-ins. Suits me. I have a husband and children waiting for me at the end of the day, and it's convenient to deal with people who go to bed when the sun goes down. Anyway, not long after Marjorie died and I went to perhaps the loveliest funeral I'd ever attended, I was struck by how funerals need more participation, and more care taken to represent the deceased.

I knew from delivering special meals to the nursing home that they're all in there talking about what they do and do not want. This one wants to be facing east so she'll see the rising sun on Judgment Day, and this other one wants to be cremated and kept in a jar at her daughter's house (whether her daughter wants that or not). This one wants "Softly and Tenderly," and that one wants "Lead on, O King Eternal." This one wants socks on her feet (poor circulation/cold extremeties), and that one wants to wear as little as possible. She's a huge woman with damp, drooping skin who says she has sweated to death here on earth and would relish the thought of being naked under some cool dirt. Pin them down and you'll find they have ideas. Pin them down good and hard, and you'll likely discover that at some point in their lives they have let their minds wander into these very specific scenes, involving death, funeral, those left behind to grieve.

Marjorie and I had sat there in her bedroom on a normal Thursday afternoon while the rest of the world was working or shopping or carpooling, and read all of her

Scriptures, sung all of her songs. At the end, she said with great joy, "I feel like I was there." She said it reminded her of being a child in her grandmother's country church, where the air smelled like the rusty pump water and the stables down the road. "It was so quiet out there," she whispered, "you could hear silence for minutes at a time, the kind of silence that makes your ears buzz and ring in the distance. It might be your own blood you're hearing. It might even be a swarm of cancer cells building a hive, but what I've always believed is what my grandmother said: a ringing in the ears is the singing of spirits." She said her half-deaf uncle said if that was so, he was the most blessed creature on earth, his dang ears had been ringing since he got too close to where some men were busting up a dam with dynamite.

"I can't believe I remembered that just now," Marjorie said, and that's when it hit me. A funeral business. People can come and have it all planned out, maybe make a video and have it put aside for later, like the will. Those who have been given a pink slip due either to diagnosis or old age, can just go right ahead and have the service, *be there*. I tried the idea out on James who, patient though he has always been, looked at me like I might have lost my mind. But there are lots of folks who are that way, those who find death too depressing.

They like the idea that it might all go away. There are those who are scared to death of death and can't bear to talk about it. Well, obviously I am not one. The day after Marjorie's funeral, I dreamed I was dying. I had less than six months to live. In my dream I was mainly sad over the fact that I would not be there to oversee my daughter's and sons' graduations from high school and college, their weddings, the grandbabies. I was worried that their father might not indulge them in the fashion of the day, which is so important when you're young, that he might not surround them with animals who might sense and alert them to things in the air. The thought of missing all of that was bad, but aside from that sadness, there was a feeling of great satisfaction. In my dream I was looking at James and the kids who were all gathered around our striped dining table to observe the electricity James could get out of a wired potato (it was a memory picture—they were much younger in the dream than in reality), and what I was feeling was peace. I thought: I have accomplished more than I ever thought I would. I have lived a good life. When I woke up I wiggled up close to James, and even though I was still crying, I had never felt more alive in my whole life. It was like the way people come out of a revival after being saved, only I knew that this was the real thing, and it has not worn off, either.

People weren't so hepped up on the funeral business to begin with, but all it took was for them to attend one or two, and then as happens in every life event, they were wanting to outdo what had already been done. Lord, people do get carried away. Now, if I let them go hog wild without monitoring, then I could not live with myself. For example, I do not let them select and order their own invitations. I take care of that myself—it's clear and functional, black print on nice white vellum: "It's a Funeral! RSVP," and then I put who it is for and the time and place. Maybe pictures of hearts or balloons. It's what I think of as the pine-box method. Everybody gets the same treatment. From there, they can add whatever they please, but what I *do* require of all of the honored guests is a speech. This is where the memories come in, the real stuff. This is where they get to say all that they want to to the world they are leaving. I encourage them to think about what they want to leave. Are there enemies you need to clear the air with? James and I have always lived by that rule of not going to bed angry. Like you might still be a little hurt or carrying a grudge but you have to look the other one in the eyes and show that there is love there, there is forgiveness.

I think the reason James is so big on this rule is because sleep death runs in his family. This is not a real disease, of course, but something I named myself. The people in James's family will just go to bed and never get up. It happened to both of his grandfathers, two uncles, and a cousin. Sleep death, like a grown up version of SIDS—it's on both sides. The poor man (though his intellectual scientific side rarely lets him admit it) goes to bed every night expecting not to wake up. I rib him about it. Of course, I have no right to make fun of him. I still get down on my knees every night and look under the bed for bogeymen—*real* bogeymen—I am much more afraid of the living than of the dead. James wonders what I'll do if I ever come face to face with one. I have had to do this ever since I learned that Charles Manson was all curled up into a kitchen cabinet when they found him. Imagine that —go after your box of Total or Froot Loops and find a filthy-headed, crazed murderer. I have always been prepared to see death. I think of it as my way of life.

In our town some have begun to call me the Mistress of Death, which makes me sound like some kind of horror show. My boys are now fourteen, and this is causing them (especially Jimmy) more grief than the bouts of acne he inherited from his father. Don't even ask what their sister thinks! Still, I cling to the knowledge that one day he will grow up and see me for what I am. An aid to the other side. A hand to hold. Now I don't want anybody thinking I am the female Kevorkian. I do not assist. There was an occasion when my radar told me loud and clear that suicide was on the woman's brain, and I did look the other way. I looked the other way, the same way I do when one of my clients has to interrupt our planning to use a bed pan or cover her face with an oxygen mask or stumble to the bathroom to be sick.

There are those who can admit to dying and those who can't. Sometimes there are those who have been given the pink slip but can't face it, so the family calls me in to make the plans. I have seen some people sit right there at their own funerals and hear the loveliest things said about them and still not comment. It's as if they are no longer there; that the soul just up and skipped out the back door when no one was looking. But then you look closer, and you see. A memory has slipped into place and locked in. I have found that many have to move backward to get through death. They need something they can count on, and the past is solid.

One of the nicest things I ever heard about someone was that when he went to his daughter's softball games he always took a cooler of water and towels for the whole team. This same man was said to have always spoken to people on the street, and to have greeted them in a way that made them feel unique and noticed on the face of the earth. He also fed stray cats and lifted birds back into their nests. And he hugged his wife and children and told them he loved them every single day. The people who have lived such a life get back a bit of the reward they have never asked for. Most are embarrassed by it, but in spite of the flush, there is great pleasure. Those who have lived a selfish, blind kind of life have a final chance to change. There was one poor woman who had herself a funeral and nobody came. It was just like in that Beatles song "Eleanor Rigby"—tragic—she sat there in front of that table laid out with some of the prettiest food I'd ever prepared and cried like she might have been five years old and nobody came to her birthday party, or like she might have been twenty and stranded at the altar. So I told her it was her practice run. Now she could write letters and notes and make phone calls and have another funeral. The next time she had a full house, and when she died for real they all came back with good memories of the last time they had seen her. They laughed about how she whipped off her wig and put it on her doctor's head, then turned her face to the sun. For a moment she looked like a character out of some kind of sci-fi movie, her head bald and her eyes bulging; she looked like a holocaust victim, an abandoned leper. She looked like death. "Why," she asked those who had gathered there, "did I waste my time being such a godawful bitch?" She laughed and said to her neighbor's child, now a grown man with three children of his own—the boy she once pinned against a fence and humiliated with criticism of his poor attire and poor manners in front of the whole neighborhood to make the point that no goddamned body was allowed to pick her flowers or shake her fruit trees—"I should have given you children those trees. I wish you had picked every peony that ever bloomed."

I have made it my business in this business to get folks as close as possible to what means the most in this life. What are your loves and what are your regrets. I tell folks that once that door opens, there's no going back. You need to shrug off the regrets. Like the gecko lizard my kids have had for a couple of years. One time, I spent a whole day watching him slip from his crusty old skin and walk away from it, leaving it to lie there like a transparent jump suit. I said to James, "God, don't you know he must feel good to shed that," and then, of course, I immediately came to understand where my grandmother had gotten her saying, "I need to get shed of that." Again and again, it's the whole birth process in motion—born again, without having to give a testimony or ask anybody's permission. Some animals turn around and eat the skin, losing absolutely nothing of what has been created.

There are those who say they don't believe in anything at all but still want to have what we jokingly call "The Going-Out Party." These are usually the young people —angry as they well should be—about getting dealt a bad hand. For these occasions I suggest songs such as Billy Joel's "Only the Good Die Young" or Queen's "Nothing Really Matters." I have found that everybody at the party, including the dying, understands that something really does matter. It might be a grandmother recalling his first time walking—a plump, diapered boy with dimpled doughy legs and sticky hands and neck that she loved so much she kissed and kissed all the day long. It might be the girl who sat behind him on the school bus every day of junior high, the way he hoped his initials would one day wind up penned on the front of her blue horse notebook; it might be a dog, long dead himself, or the one curled at his feet, those somber, liquid brown eyes filled with knowledge and loss. Even if they continue to believe that nothing waits beyond, they are reassured that things in life do matter—every day, every word, every strain of music, every little gust of wind that stirs the branches.

It was after one of these parties for someone young that I was asked questions. The young man, for whom I had thrown a humdinger of a party, would not be lingering for much longer. His eyes reminded me of my daughter's eyes. His hands were pale and graceful like Marjorie's. I heard my own sons in his language, and I heard James in his lengthy sighs.

"Nice cake," he said, pointing to what remained. I had felt Marjorie's hand guiding me as I constructed a closet, solid brown chocolate as it should be with its door cracked open to let all the life come out: Barbie in a swimsuit and Magic Earring Ken, a parade of tiny plastic high heels; perfect pink triangles of frosting around the base. I had heard several people (older relatives) say that they didn't understand the cake, only to be pulled over to the side by someone in the know. He had told me he had no regrets about his choices, just about the bad luck that got factored in. After his party he asked me to open *my* file cabinet for him; he asked *me* to tell *him* a secret.

The secret that I told him was that before and after every dinner party I go through my house with a smudge stick like a torch. I do it while James is in the shower and won't know about it. He always comes out, sniffs and says, "What's that I smell?" and I say something like "your upper lip." I don't tell him that I am casting a spell to rid our house of bad vibes and whatever bitterness a soul like that of the OB might leave, a wake of stench behind him. I don't tell him that I am still sometimes overcome with guilt over my one and only affair, a crazy brief meeting with a childhood boyfriend who had lost a parent as recently as I had. Grief is a passion even stronger than lust, and those who don't recognize it will eventually shatter and spray blood and bone to kingdom come. I am still burning a little in guilt for loving every minute of that time and the way it took years off of my heart. But never, in my mind, did it feel like something that could jeopordize my love for James. In my mind it brought my two halves together and linked them up like two full and heavy train cars getting ready for the long haul.

I told the young man that if James knew I buy smudge sticks by the case, he'd say what he always says, that I'm crazy and superstitious and he cannot remember why he married me. Of course, that *is* a joke—'long about midnight he remembers well enough. "Now that's some magic," he might say, and I just laugh, when in my head I'm thinking *that*'s biology; magic is beyond us. It's in that flicker of light in my linden tree on an autumn day so crisp and clean I feel I could leap right up into that tree and sit like a bird for the rest of my life. Magic is when I hear the very song on the radio that I just wished to hear or when I get a check in the mail on the very day I say I sure could use one. Usually it's a joke check—like the last time I asked for money and got a check for twelve dollars for overpaying my bill at Sears. Still, seek and ye shall find—ask, and it shall be given. I can forsake a lot of the Baptist business I grew up with, but there are those scriptures that remain in my head as if they are carved there. Sometimes, I get magic and religion mixed up in my head. I guess of the two I have to choose magic—or call it spiritual. Sometimes, when I'm riding in the car all by myself, I'll suddenly breathe in the smell of rich sweet pipe tobacco and believe that were I tempted, I could glance in the rearview mirror and see my grandfather there; it's so real to me that I never look, for fear that when I do see him I'll wreck the car.

I was only ten when he died, but I believe I helped him over to the other side. He was pointing over to the corner of the room, saying that he needed to go there. When all the grown-ups left, I helped him slide to the hardwood floor where he sat on the top sheet, and then I pulled him over there. I pulled fast, like a sled dog, because the adults would be returning with pills and doctors. I pulled harder and faster, as fast as I could and when I got him to the corner, he smiled, first at me and then into and all around the corner. He never looked back, and when the adults found me there, crouched beside him, they became hysterical. They brought it up time and time again over the years. And when they did, I allowed myself to slip away to something better—warm sunshine on a summer afternoon, the baked brick stoop of my grandfather's porch, where I waited for him to come and pull me inside to the cool darkness of his tobacco-drenched house.

As I went on and on, I realized that I was planning my own funeral, cheese and johnny cakes like you can't find anymore, such old hymns as "Sweet By and By," mixed in with a little Sinatra—"When You're Smiling"—and some Louis Armstrong—"Sittin' in the Sun" or "What a Wonderful World"—and it is, or at least it could be, should be, can be. People keep forgetting that and giving up, but it ain't over until it's over. My dogs seem to know that; they sniff the good pure air and stretch out in a puddle of sunshine. I decide to think about my guest list and who all would be there: cat, dog, and human, some living and some dead. I think of a little speech given by a man not too long ago, when his mind was cloudy with morphine and fatigue. He had planned a lovely speech about his family, his pets, his coworkers down at the garage, but at the last minute he said he wanted to talk about the new tax laws. He said first of all that this new law dealt with each and every person in the exact same way; there is no distinction or special consideration for any one group over another one. He said if the laws are working and people are feeling hopeful, then that is good—trust them, believe in them, stick with them—oh, but if you see that they are not going to work, then you have to accept that. You have to embrace that truth and then find another way to go. When he stopped talking, his yard was silent; there was bewilderment and then there were nods as slowly his metaphor settled gently over us. I reached and took James's hand and squeezed it, just as I reached to take the hand of the young man beside me. His fingers were mottled and cold. My ears rang with the power of silence, which I recognized as a sign, and I knew that it was a good one.

The Anatomy of Man

It was with trepidation that he took the first dip in the baptismal pool. He eased in slowly, the white cotton of his robe billowing around him like a cloud. He had made the water warm, soothing. From the pool, he looked out at the rows upon rows of empty pews, heard the silence. With that silence came freedom. He did the breaststroke and backstroke. *Immersion.*

Now it's part of his routine.

The office staff members shake their heads in wonder at the young pastor who never seems to tire. "I'll stay if you need me," the secretary says. She is middle aged. Her head of blond hair gives—from a distance—the appearance of a much younger person. Her offer is sincere. She often speaks of the difficulties of going home to an empty house. "I don't mean it's difficult for you, dear," she says. "I mean for those of us who once had very full houses." She draws nods from several of the other women, volunteers there to help out with the newsletter. He once admitted he'd like to have a full house himself someday, and now he is offered photographs: daughters, granddaughters, nieces—*good girls.*

He sends her away and as the halls empty and darken and the custodian turns the last key in the last lock, he finds his way to the sanctuary, strips, and steps in. He floats. It is his meditation chamber.

Baptist/Methodist/Catholic/Jew/Whatever. He could be any, or all. But he has chosen what comes most naturally. He has fallen back on the knowledge of his childhood. He has brought to it his experiences from beyond. He has loved this place. He has felt both beckoned and rejected; understood and grossly misjudged.

Early in his childhood there was a pushing and a pulling, a twisting and a whispering. He did not think of it as religious. It was what he *knew* about things—a darkness, a brightness. And he knew better as a child than to tell anyone.

He had a great-uncle who could see germs lit up like infrared. He saw them where ever he looked. They were on doorknobs, food, human hands. He believed his uncle even as he watched him taken away for heavy medication and arts and crafts lessons. Now there are other places to turn.

In high school, he once saw a man in the checkout line at a supermarket, whose breath labored and caught each time his chest expanded. He'd gone for hot dogs and chips to take on a camping trip. He'd go next to a neighboring county to buy beer. He'd sleep with his first girlfriend and promise her things he knew he would never give her. Waiting in the checkout line, he heard the man cough and saw the cancer cells. They were not unlike his uncle's description of the germs. They swam through the man's bloodstream, little twigs tossed into a current. Does it wash eternally or does it catch and snag without warning, embedded in the fleshy bank only to grow, metastasize? Beckoned through the big glass window by his crowd of restless friends he took his change, said his thanks, and ran out into a day wild with life. He felt lifted above it all a bit. He hovered just high enough to glimpse the edge.

The man whose cancer cells he'd seen was the husband of a woman who worked in the school cafeteria. When the man died, he snuck away and stood at the back of the crowd at the graveside service. People remarked what a kind boy he was. His mother repeated these compliments. What she said made his skin crawl. He wondered if there might have been something he could have done that day in the checkout line to change the course of things.

Now he floats on his back, arms and legs spread. He stares at the stained glass above him. Against a solid wall, it is illuminated from behind with electric light and gives the effect of eternal sunshine. There kneels Jesus holding a lamb close to his chest. *I am the life. I am the life.* He holds his position, letting the words filter. He thinks of the crucifixion. He thinks of da Vinci's *Anatomy of Man.* He thinks of William Holden facedown in the pool in *Sunset Boulevard.* The point-of-view problem always bothers him —narration by a dead man. So? Call it the resurrected voice. The movie is too good to reject. The afterlife. He thinks of Jay Gatsby floating in *his* pool.

He imagines he hears one of the big front doors opening. Impossible. Churches are no longer left unlocked. They offer no place for the weary to creep and take refuge. If the door were left unlocked, there'd be people huddled in the vestibule, carts from Winn-Dixie parked outside, greasy paper sacks with scraps of food, Merita bread bags knotted like purses, torn blankets mildewed and lice-infected.

Why *is* he here, locked inside?

Marianne was sixteen when he was eight. She was the girl next door. He marveled at her high school life. She invited him to sit and listen to her records while her world spun in fast gear. He loved her in her cut-off jeans, great big rollers in her hair until the very last minute when her boyfriend rang the doorbell. He was told to ask the boyfriend to sit down and wait. And then she would appear, the perfect vision of what a girl should be, in her miniskirt and draped sweater. Her dark hair reached her waist. It swung as she walked away. It was the end of summer. She had wanted to hear "See You in September" over and over. It had been his job to lift the arm of the record player and put it back in the first groove of the forty-five. She ruffled his hair in passing, told him what great eyelashes he had—*a girl would just die for those!* He loved her. She was beautiful. When he watched her walk away, he saw her shrouded in darkness, a cloak of sadness that settled and stuck, its edges limned in sparkling light.

The women he wants, the women who spark his blood, shy away from him. Does a commitment to God mean he can't be choosy? Can't wish for sleek bare skin, sweat and leather? Didn't David choose Bathsheba? He murdered to get her. Imagine David on trial. He didn't kill *directly,* his lawyer might say. Convict this one of manslaughter. And what of Abraham, who carried Isaac off to the mountain to murder him for God. Wouldn't Abraham be proclaimed psychotic and hauled off for heavy medication and lessons in arts and crafts?

One woman in the congregation cannot look him in the eye. He can see her unhappiness, feel it, when her slick young husband, a deacon, slips into the pew beside her and she sits rigidly. She is someone in need of salvation, but what attention does she get? It's not her soul that is in doubt but her everyday life, approved and blessed by all.

He thinks of her often. Just try to stop the thoughts from coming. Surely King David was no stranger to such thoughts. Surely everyone has a fantasy? His is that she appears at the baptismal in a white bikini and steps in. Her red toenails—blood red burgundy—with lips to match are the crimson of communion wine, her skin as papery white and fragile as the unleavened wafers. He tells her that he can make her weep with joy; he can teach her to speak in foreign tongues. Then she pours out a confession to him that freezes his blood. She might then as well be an old woman shriveled with age. He changes the setting, finds a Jacuzzi in a tropical resort for the two of them, but he hears coughs all around him. He can see infrared germs. There is a deep wash of sadness.

Dear God.

As a boy he had played a game at church. The rules: open the hymnal and read every title adding "in bed." Just As I Am in Bed. How Great Thou Art in Bed. Blessed Be the Tie that Binds in Bed. Love Lifted Me in Bed.

The church doors should be opened. Charity begins at home. Charity is color-blind. Charity does not attach strings. His arguments are lost in the shuffle. In the past there has been vandalism. They need to build new buildings, not spend money reclaiming the ones they already have. They need new buses and paved courtyards.

When he was in college and planning to teach religion, he met a self-proclaimed preacher who paced the brick pit in front of the student union like an animal. He wore a terry cloth robe of many colors and condemned his hecklers to hell. By the end of a week he had condemned everyone to hell who had not added their names to his meager little list of disciples; by then it was public knowledge that the preacher's robe came from an expensive men's store in the mall and that the preacher's Porsche was parked over on the far side of downtown, so that everyone would think that he had walked into town from Jerusalem when instead he had driven in from another state where he lived in an expensive condominium.

Be ye not deceived, he had whispered to his girlfriend, a sorority girl who loved nothing better than to shag, drink beer, and laugh at his dirty jokes.

The story of Joseph was his favorite. The forgiveness Joseph gave to his brothers, the love of Joseph's father, the mystical aspect of the story, Joseph's visions and dreams, and the way his brothers turned against him. They didn't want to hear that the sheaves they had bound in the field bowed down to his; they would rather sell Joseph off to the Egyptians. As a graduate student he had written a paper about dysfunction in biblical lines; about how revising it, straightening it out, so that everybody did the right thing, you'd have a very different story. If Abraham hadn't scared the hell out of Isaac, Isaac might not have been the same fellow, might not have wound up with Jacob and Esau (another story to prove that the world is not always just given that Jacob got where he got by betraying his father into giving up his brother's birthright). But if not for that weakness, Jacob might not have learned what he did when he was forgiven by Esau, might not have had the sons he did, including Joseph. And so on. You cannot untangle one line from another; it just keeps reaching and reaching to who begat whom and how it all occurred.

Was that what led him here, to this profession, to this town? There was no significant moment that turned him this way; rather, it was a lifetime of little choices and movements. The thought *a hiding place* comes to mind; words like *sanctuary* reinforce the idea that he can lead a sheltered and protected life and still reach out to other places in life. A double life. A split life. Has that concept always been in place?

His childhood hiding place was inside an old-fashioned wardrobe in the guest room. The piece was (in his mother's words) an eyesore, but because it had a family history, she kept it. It smelled of cedar and mothballs, and he liked to sit on a folded quilt his grandmother had made from gray and black flannel, scraps of clothing from men long deceased. His mother called it the funeral quilt, but in the darkness of the wardrobe with a sliver of light coming through the crack in the door, it was a comforting quilt. He liked to sit for long periods of time until his forehead perspired and he got drowsy. Only then would he swing the door open and suck in a wonderful breath of fresh air, and squint against the afternoon sunlight that filled that room at the back of his mother's house. The room had once been a porch and still had a tin roof. The memory of rain falling on that roof lulls him into a great sense of peace. It is a feeling much like what he feels floating here on his back, his ears immersed so that every thought keeps rhythm with the beating of his own heart.

Once, he kicked open the wardrobe door and jumped into the room to find his uncle perched on the edge of the bed, his hands clasped and wringing. The relatives were already saying, "He'll have to go back."

"Abracadabra," his uncle said. "I made a boy appear."

He laughed and moved to the bed when his uncle patted the space beside him. It seemed they sat there for a long time without speaking, and then his uncle began to talk in a low whisper. It wasn't fair for him to be tapped into so much knowledge, he said. To be chosen in such a way is, he said, both a blessing and a curse. *Ignorance is bliss,* he whispered and bent down close. His eyes were like a cat's—amber, like something prehistoric. His uncle spent much of his life studying maps and could name every capital and country; he knew populations, and he knew the average temperatures and what pests (killer bees, poisonous snakes and spiders) plagued each place. Visitors were often entertained by his knowledge and found him quite charming. And he was, it was true, very handsome—tall and lean, with his dark, curly hair and amber eyes. People quizzed him, tried to stump him on this capital or that; his uncle was never stumped. But inevitably he would turn with a look of horror and point out into the yard or up at the ceiling or at the scalp of the visitor. *My God,* he would mutter and step back. Then he would describe what he saw in great detail.

Should I deny what I see as truth? his uncle asked him that day when they sat side by side on the bed. *Should I pretend that none of what I see and hear is happening?* His uncle searched his expression then the same way he searched his maps, committing to memory every pore on his face. It was as if his uncle was reading him. "You believe me, don't you?" his uncle whispered. How could he not believe him?

Now as he floats he pictures his uncle's much older, tormented face. These days there would be medicine. These days he would not have (as his relatives say) *crossed the line,* or if he did cross it they would be able to call him back. All those years his uncle remembered his face; his uncle remembered the day that he leapt from the cedar wardrobe into the light of day. He would say, *I know you.* He would say, *You believe me, don't you?* And wasn't his uncle right about so much? *People do not wash their hands,* his uncle had whispered to him once when the grownups were pretending he wasn't there. *The human touch can be a deadly thing.*

Marianne walks into this church one Sunday morning. Her skin has aged, damp and soured, as if alcohol seeps from every pore. As he speaks (youth group car wash and cookout in the park) he grieves at her spidery arms, white and heavily veined; at her dress that is too large and hangs from her shoulders like an old rag. What he heard is that she has never gotten her life on track—one bad choice begetting another. He'd sung along with her to her stack of forty-fives. Everything about her seemed perfect. Now he turns his gaze to a young woman near the front, her perfect suit, shoes, hair, makeup, the big man beside her stretching himself, one fancy foot in the aisle, arms claiming the whole pew. What a fine line we all walk. She is perched and waiting. Fly, fall, or simply wait in sadness?

After the service he stands down front and waits while Marianne moves toward him. He steps forward to meet her and hugs her close, her bony chest fragile and raspy. He could squeeze her to death with very little effort. He smells her fear and desperation as he holds her close, perhaps too close. The music director stares. The music director has very strict opinions about what is suitable. Clapping in church is a sin, for example, and women should not bring children into the sanctuary unless they can behave and sit quietly and silently. One of these times he will turn and agree with her and get everyone's attention. He will say, "If Jesus were here he would take that child outside and wear his butt out. Jesus would knock some manners into him, wouldn't he?"

"Suffer the children," she will say, with smug authority, flat lips cutting a straight line across her broad face. "To come unto me."

"Yes," he will answer. "Could you translate?"

"Make them behave before they come to my house of worship!"

"What about *let* them come, *allow* them to come?"

You can't always believe what people say, his uncle whispered. *People will ask that you believe the strangest things.*

"So how do you know what to believe?" he had asked, and his uncle laughed. He laughed until tears ran from his eyes, until a team of nurses dashed in to check his restraints, afraid he would rip out his oxygen and IV line again. And what was in the laughter? Was he saying, "What? You're asking me, the family nutcase?" Or was the laughter saying, "Such a silly, silly question." The only time his uncle mentioned religion was when he once recalled with great fondness a girl he liked in junior high school, back in the days when he was a quiet, studious boy without any idea of what lay ahead of him. The girl, his uncle told him, always wore socks that matched her sweater, and she drove three towns over on Friday nights for services. She played Torah Tic-Tac-Toe and Hebrew baseball, which the uncle said sounded about like those old Bible drills he hated. He said she spoke just enough Hebrew to set his heart on fire.

Marianne steps back. "We're so proud of you," she says, her quiet voice as broken as her body.

He pulls her back close again, and to the shock of the music director and all of the choir members clustered about and all of the children clamoring to ask if they can bring friends to the cookout—*absolutely*—he kisses her forehead, cheeks, nose, lips. He holds her hands and kisses them, opens her sweaty palms and takes the bulletin folded and wadded there. "I always loved you," he says. "My dream girl," he tells the group around him. "A young boy's perfect dream."

Now as he floats, drifting in and out of sleep, he feels unworthy. He feels like a failure, someone who somewhere along the line has stopped paying attention. *It is important that I DO something,* his uncle had cried when they found him burning the field to rid it of swarms of flies, possibly killer bees, maybe even locusts. *If you don't do something,* he said, *your beliefs are worthless.*

"Why am I here?" he asks now, once again looking up to the stained glass.

"That's what I'd like to know."

The voice comes from nowhere and fills the room. He stands, the water up to his chest. He is aware of his nakedness under the loose robe but feels no compulsion to hide. There is a long awkward silence, during which he is already planning where he will go, what he will do. He will have to leave this place, and then maybe he will change professions. Maybe he'll finally get a life and a sex life to go with it—a real one—no participation of the Holy Spirit, no ghosts of disease and depression. He knows all that he needs to know.

"Do things," the voice says. "Keep the doors open."

He nods, mouths his thanks. Then waits for more instructions. He will leave blankets in the vestibule. He will leave food, water, books, soap, towels, toothbrushes, clean clothes. He will leave toys, puzzles. When the voice does not continue, he takes a deep breath and dives to the bottom of the baptismal—*immersion.* He enters darkness, only to burst back into life and light and air. *Be ye not deceived,* his uncle once whispered while drawing the United States with his eyes closed. *It's all much simpler than it looks.*